ALL NIGHT LONG

O'GALLAGHER NIGHTS

BRENNA STONE

MIGNON MYKEL

Also By Mignon Mykel

LOVE IN ALL PLACES *series*
full series reading order

Interference **(Prescott Family)**
O'Gallagher Nights: The Complete Series
Troublemaker **(Prescott Family)***
Saving Grace **(Loving Meadows)**
Breakaway **(Prescott Family)***
Altercation **(Prescott Family)***
27: Dropping the Gloves **(Enforcers of San Diego)**
32: Refuse to Lose **(Enforcers of San Diego)**
Holding **(Prescott Family)***
A Holiday for the Books **(Prescott Family)**
25: Angels and Assists **(Enforcers of San Diego)**
From the Beginning **(Prescott Family)**

ALL NIGHT LONG

O'GALLAGHER NIGHTS

BRENNA STONE

MIGNON MYKEL

ISBN-13: 978-1539447498
ISBN-10: 1539447499

Cover and Formatting: oh so Novel
Editor: Jenn Wood
All images and vectors have been purchased

O'GALLAGHER NIGHTS SERIES

One Night Stand
About Last Night
All Night Long
Hot Holiday Nights: Rory and Emily

PROLOGUE

For as long as I could remember, I've lived under the protective shadow of my older brothers. We were all fairly spread apart in age, at least in comparison to my friends who were one or two years, three years at most, apart from the other kids in their families.

But for my brothers and me? We had the four-year gap.

Well, technically Rory and Conor were three years apart but their birthdates were on opposite ends of the year.

So pretty much four years.

That meant I never went to the same school as Conor, who is eight years older than me.

It also meant that there had only been two years in elementary school, no years in middle school, and one four-quarter period in in the space of life that was known as high school, that I had with Rory.

That did not stop the two of them from threatening every kid they ran across though.

People knew who I was.

If there were such a thing in our little beach town, I would have been considered royalty with the way my brothers watched over me.

By ten—ten!—I decided I needed to find a way to step away from the pampered role everyone saw me in, so I set out to do just that.

Away from my brothers' eyes, of course.

Which only made their unwavering faith in me feel like a dagger through the heart, with every omission of truth I told them. Or the little parts of my life that I didn't tell them. The little parts that made the large sum of who I was.

The things that they considered rumors.

I pushed away good friends so I could fit in.

I'm ashamed to say I spread my legs to ruin that 'good girl' reputation my brothers molded for me.

By day, I was Sweet Brenna O'Gallagher, the girl who could do no wrong in her brothers' eyes.

But everyone else knew who I really was.

They knew the slutty girl, the one who wore low cut tops and too much eye makeup.

The girl who was known behind hands as the one who fucked a senior in his van her freshman year.

Then rumors spread about other things.

STDs. Drugs. Pregnancies.

While most of those rumors I could give a big 'fuck you' to, there was one rumor that hit incredibly close to home, one that wasn't a rumor at all.

And every time I heard it, every time I saw someone whispering behind their hands, their eyes avoiding mine but looking for the tell-tale signs, the pain in my gut, in my heart, was so incredibly agonizing that I could not bear to be that person anymore.

So I vowed off men the year I turned nineteen.

Nineteen.

The time most girls were starting to find who they were.

I had already found who I was and I didn't like her. I didn't like what she did to her body, what she did to her head, what she did to her heart.

I was successful at keeping men at bay for two years. Granted, the rumors turned into 'cock tease' but that was infinitely better than what they had been.

For two years, my vow of celibacy, of staying away from men, wasn't even tempted to change. But then my brothers hired him.

Greyson Stone.

Stone to everyone. Grey to just me.

Behind closed doors.

Behind our hands. Away from public. Away from my brothers.

Just like every other aspect of who I truly was, I was extremely good at hiding this relationship from my brothers.

But Grey was threatening to change that.

Five years, he let me have him in secret.

Five years, and he knew who I really was, who I hid from my brothers. He knew and he wanted to expose me.

Expose us.

So what could I do but try and push him away?

CHAPTER ONE

BRENNA

I walked into the pub that had been as much a part of my life as the family home had been, ready for my first shift working under my brothers' reign.

Conor and Rory re-opened the doors to our parents' pub last year, but between my age and, let's be honest, the desire to not work for my brothers, I respectfully declined every offer they gave me to be a barmaid.

A barmaid!

In my family's bar!

Just call me Cinderella, then.

At least give me a good job. Books or something. Don't make me start from the ground when the two of them were just...handed the place!

They saw me as some weak creature in their world, but I suppose some of that was my own fault. They often mistook my pain of the rumors that swirled about me as just that—pain of rumors—when in all actuality, the pain was because the truth they all spewed.

But I needed a job and this was one I didn't have to apply for.

I did the community college thing after high school. My brothers thought I got a 'feel good' degree, an associate degree in something like graphic design or something, but really I was now the proud owner of an Associate Degree in Business Management.

I was keeping that card close to my chest though.

I did also have some graphic design knowledge because come on, my brothers thought I was taking the classes—I had to actually take some.

I may not be telling them about my business knowledge anytime soon, I wanted to learn the ins and outs of our particular setting before I showed my hand, but I could at least prove my worth with menu and ad design.

If they let me.

In the meantime though, I was going to do the Cinderella thing and wait tables because goodness knew, my brothers didn't want me to even think about getting my bartending license until I was twenty-one.

The law was twenty-one, yeah, but I could at least start looking at the materials.

This bubble they put me under?

It effing sucked.

But I went with the flow, letting them think whatever they wanted to think because that's what I did best. It's what made me...me.

Through the back door, I stepped into the kitchen and made my way to the office. There were pegs and lockers for other staff members, but Conor told me I could use the office with him and Rore.

It was early yet, ten on a Friday morning. O'Gallaghers wouldn't open for another hour and even then, it wouldn't be hopping. The kitchen was devoid of people, but I could hear some sounds.

At first I thought maybe Rory turned on a game in the bar, but as I neared the office, I realized the sounds were coming from in there. Voices.

Two of the voices I recognized as my brothers.

The other was unfamiliar. It wasn't as low as Conor's, but certainly wasn't a high pitched voice, either. It was a 'just right' kind of voice, the type that you knew would whisper gruffly in your ear one moment, and laugh jovially with you the next.

Not that I had any recent experience.

I walked into the office, realizing that my brothers were currently interviewing this beautiful voice.

Or had been.

The three of them were all smiling and laughing now.

"Morning boys," I said, walking into the room.

The laughing faces all turned toward me, and Conor, in his office chair with his hands on his belly, grinned wide behind his beard. He started wearing it when he was seventeen; I don't remember what he looked like without it anymore.

"Morning, Brenna. Stone, this is Bren, our sister. Brenna, Greyson Stone."

Stone stood from his chair and stepped forward with one foot, closing the small distance between us in a respectable way, still close enough to his chair that he could sit after introducing himself to me.

With his hand held out, he flashed me a beautifully crooked smile, showing off straight white teeth in his square jaw. "Stone."

I gave him a welcoming smile, taking his hand in mine. "Nice to meet you. Brenna." I took in his clear, clear gray eyes. I had only ever seen the clearness in blue, the type of color you felt you could see right through.

But Stone's gray eyes...

I could fall in the never ending clear depths.

I mentally shook myself.

I was done with men. Falling for this one wouldn't do me any good.

Besides, my brothers probably gave him an ultimatum.

"You as well," he said, pulling me from my thoughts. I slid my hand from his and smiled wide toward my brothers as Stone sat again.

Rory, at twenty-five, was finally growing out of his baby looks and looking like a real live adult. If only he acted like one.

"What would you boys like for me to do?" I went to the filing cabinet, opening the bottom drawer in the metal monstrosity. I grimaced at the scratch of metal on metal. This beast was here when I was a baby.

I dropped my purse into the empty drawer and faced my brothers again.

"We're just about done here with Stone. He's our new bartender. He'll be working with me and you this afternoon," Conor said. I often felt that while this whole re-opening adventure was credited to both Conor and Rory, Conor was the one manning the expedition. Rory simply stood back and was a presence.

"In the meantime, if you want to get glasses set, that would be a great help."

"Sure thing." I turned back to the door to leave. I almost stopped to say something to Stone, something along the lines of 'nice to meet you,' but thought better of it.

Especially seeing as he and I would be working together.

Today.

I was going to have to repeat my no-men mantra over and over today, there wasn't a doubt in my mind.

STONE

I tried to watch Brenna leave from the corner of my eye.

One of the first warnings I received was that the youngest O'Gallagher was starting today too, and that she was strictly off limits, which only made me want to meet her more.

I knew she was going to be gorgeous.

Her brothers weren't bad looking dudes, so I had a feeling she was going to be right up there with them. I wasn't prepared for the knock I received when she walked into the office, all raven-colored, wavy hair and bright smile. Her eyes were green and stood out against her face, framed by thick dark eyelashes.

She was one of the most gorgeous women I ever had the pleasure of laying my eyes on. Staying away from her, on a personal level, was definitely going to be a challenge.

"So, we good?" Rory asked Conor. The kid looked like he had other places to be.

Conor nodded. "Sure, yeah. If you could just work on coming up with promotional things, that'd be great."

"Will do. Great meeting you, Stone. Look forward to working with you." Rory slid past the desk, seemingly in a hurry to leave.

When he left, Conor shook his head with a chuckle. "That kid. I swear—the actual act of working would kill him. But he's pretty brilliant on the other side of things."

I offered a crooked grin. "It's the age. You're either ready or you're not." Like Rory, I was twenty-five, but I definitely thought I was more adult than he was. The way he dressed stated he cared a great deal about what people thought. The way he held himself gave off the vibe that he put himself higher than others. And there was nothing wrong with any of that; everyone's experiences shaped them differently.

Mine just included a dad who beat on me until my mom got the courage for us to leave when I was thirteen. You grew up fast in that life and learned that appearances were rarely what they seemed.

"You need to do anything, grab anything, before hitting the floor?" Conor asked as he stood from the desk. I took that as my cue to stand as well, more than ready to get started. I didn't like sitting around doing nothing. I preferred being active as many hours of the day as possible.

I hadn't gone to college so my options for working tended to be on the slimmer side. I started bartending at twenty-one, at a pretty busy bar downtown. Found I loved not just the atmosphere, but talking to the people. Some places were better than others, sure. One of the reasons I left the other bar was because a friend and I had come to this one a few months ago and I fell for the aura of the place. It was modern yet rustic. Hip but had a huge range of patrons.

I'd been at the other bar for two years but was ready for a change. I left on good terms, something that was incredibly important to me.

I didn't believe in burning bridges.

You never knew when you'd need one of them again.

I had already done a walk-through of the pub when I first arrived, so Conor simply led me into the main bar area. I glanced at a table where Brenna was wrapping silverware and occasionally glancing up toward the TV. There was a hockey game on and I was impressed to see she was actually paying attention to it.

"The Enforcers have made this place their spot," Conor said, nodding toward the television. "Occasionally we'll see a Padres player or a Charger, but the place is almost always littered with hockey players." He moved toward the end of the bar, where the coolers and such were. "When you're on, feel free to organize all this however works best for you." He went to one of the chests and pulled out empty containers, as well as a few that were covered. He took the covers off and revealed lemons, olives, and other condiments.

"I'll leave you to this. Have some book work to do and need to get your paperwork submitted. You good?"

I nodded, stuffing the tips of my fingers into the pockets of my jeans. "Absolutely."

Conor nodded once and moved past me, clapping me on the shoulder. "Good to have you here."

As I began to prep the bar to my liking, I kept an ear on the game over my shoulder and an eye on the black-haired beauty semi-in front of me. She really was fucking gorgeous.

She had that classically beautiful face, the type that you couldn't tell if she wore makeup or not. Her lips were the perfect cupid's bow and her nose was a smaller, daintier version of the one that was on both Rory and Conor's faces.

She wore a tight O'Gallaghers shirt that showed off her ample chest. She was large on top but didn't look disproportionate. Her legs were encased in skin-tight skinny jeans and on her feet were heels.

She was wearing heels to a bar.

To work.

Her feet were going to kill her before the night was over. I chuckled and shook my head which, while not my intention, caught her attention.

Her eyes narrowed. "What's funny?"

I shook my head. "Nothing. I was just thinking to myself."

She nodded upward once, slowly, her eyes assessing me. "Sure…"

Still grinning, I looked down and started cutting lemons and limes, the sizes perfectly similar. I heard as Brenna stood and gathered her box of wrapped silverware, just as I heard her heels clicking to the back of the bar where she deposited them in what I assumed was the basket that housed them.

Her clicking moved and glancing to my left, I saw that she moved to a lower fridge. She was kneeling now, her knees to her chest as she went through the fridge.

She glanced over at me with just her eyes before turning her entire head.

"Do you have a problem?"

The left side of my face was tight in a crooked grin. I turned my attention back to my task. "Nope."

The door to the refrigeration unit shut with a solid thump and her clicking came close. It was difficult, but I kept my attention on task even though I could smell the vanilla peppermint combination of what had to be her soap or shampoo. There was no way that was a perfume.

She smelled sweet.

I had the feeling that sweet wasn't who she was.

I continued my task even though I could feel her standing next to me, facing me, staring at me. I scooped up the last of my slices and deposited them in the tub before grabbing a towel and wiping my hands. I stuffed an end of the fabric into my back pocket and turned toward her.

Her arms were over her chest and her chin and nose were both angled up. Her body language said she was impatient with me, annoyed with me, but her eyes…

The green emeralds shining up at me showed she was intrigued, but more than that?

Curious. Want. Need.

And maybe a hint of timidity.

"What's your problem?" she asked.

I mirrored her body, my arms crossed over my chest. Her eyes flickered to my forearms which were now exposed. When we were in the office earlier, the sleeves of my shirt were down but now after working with my hands, I pushed the sleeves of my long-sleeved tee up, exposing the intricate colorful designs on both.

I nodded down toward her feet. "You work a bar in those before?"

She scoffed at me, shifting ever so slightly in her spot. "No. But they are my shoe of choice and I've worn them for hours on end. What I wear on my feet should be no concern of yours."

I just grinned at her attitude. "Sure thing. Just don't come crying to me when your feet kill."

"I don't go crying to anyone."

I simply stared at her. I heard a world of truth in her words and damn if that didn't make me want to be the person she could come crying to.

Damn. Hold up.

I just met this girl and received the equivalent of a death threat from her brothers if I touched her.

Yet I didn't seem to care.

"Oh, but you will."

"Will I?" She lifted a perfectly shaped brow in challenge.

I leaned down and in so we were nearly nose to nose.

She was easily six inches shorter than me in her heels, which had to put her at around five-three without. "I think you will."

She stared at me, her face tilted up and her expression unwavering. From here, I could see gold specks in her eyes. There was a light dusting of freckles over the bridge of her nose.

And those lips of hers.

That cupid bow mouth with a plump lower lip.

They were begging to be kissed.

She smelled sweet and looked it too, and I knew without a doubt I would have this woman—someway, somehow.

In secret, in public, I didn't care.

I was making it my mission to win her over, her brothers be damned.

CHAPTER TWO

BRENNA

When I say that keeping Stone at arm's length was difficult, I mean it was the equivalent of trying to keep a ticking bomb—with a remote detonator you did not have—from going off.

For a year I managed to avoid his advances.

Hardly.

Instead, I flirted back with him, trying to prove to him just where his place was. I was the sister of his bosses and he wasn't getting anywhere with me.

Even if I wanted those thick, colorful arms around me.

His spicy, musky cologne near me.

His beautifully crooked smile aimed at me.

Stone and I fell into an easy rhythm, which turned out to be incredibly important, as he and I worked many shifts together. He may have flirted with every person with tits, but he saved a special brand of flirting just for me.

Just as I did for him.

With it, I found myself having an absurd amount of fun with him. I looked forward to working with him for more than his good looks, but for the way he made me feel.

"Hey, gorgeous. What've you got for me?" Stone said, moving down the bar to where I set my tray down to remove old bottles and glasses. Today he wore a light blue shirt that had his gray eyes popping, but I tried to not focus on that, instead focusing on work.

"I need you—"

"I've been waiting for that." His grin was smug.

I lifted a brow. "*I need you,*" I started again, "to pour me a house lager, please...oh kind sir," I added with a hint of sass. I couldn't stop the corners of my lips from angling up.

"Anything for you." He wiped his hands on the towel hanging from his side before doing just that. He glanced past me to the kitchen door before lowering his voice, speaking from the side. "When are you going to agree to go out with me?"

Every shift, without fail, he asked.

Every shift, without fail, I told him no.

But it was getting harder.

"When the sky turns orange." Still though, I smiled, watching as his large, capable hands worked the tap system.

"I heard a storm is coming. It may turn orange before you know it." He smirked, placing the glass on my tray.

"Don't hold your breath." I couldn't wipe the silly grin from my face though, even if the entire thing baffled me.

I didn't get it.

How did one manage to go two years without finding any guy attractive, only to be blindsided by someone who was technically off limits in every sense?

I didn't want a man in my life. I was tired of being that Brenna.

On top of that, I had two very protective older brothers.

Stone didn't have a chance.

But good God, I wanted him like I wanted my next breath.

Generally, my shift ended before Stone's, but for whatever reason, today he left the floor at the same time I did.

"Rory's covering for me," he said when I slid him a side glance. He followed me to the back and I almost expected him to follow me into the office as well when I went to grab my purse, but he didn't.

He was waiting by the back door, though. "So that sky? It's kind of orange right now. You see, Bren," he said, his eyes locked on mine as I neared the door and therefore, him, "regardless of a bad storm, the sky turns orange at night with the setting sun. I think you wanted to go out with me."

I continued walking toward him, slipping past him when he held the door open for me.

I may have brushed my arm along his stomach in doing so. Maybe.

Not on purpose though.

...but maybe, yeah.

"I meant green." I tried not to chuckle.

"Ah-ah, you can't go back on it." He was behind me and, without touching me, moved his arm over my shoulder and pointed toward the horizon.

O'Gallaghers may have been in a fairly populated place, but you could still make out the ocean horizon. And just past the ink marring the space beside me, just beyond the finger he pointed, was one of the most gorgeous sunsets I had the pleasure of viewing from this spot.

"Orange." His voice was low and dangerously close to my ear. "You owe me a date." He dropped his arm back to his side and I was surprised that I missed the almost contact.

There was no point fighting something that I wanted, something that I craved. I could be proud of myself for holding off men for two-plus years, and this particular one for twelve months.

I hoped like hell I was safe from disappointment though— that I learned something from my time being single.

One date.

I didn't have to sleep with him, much like I would have had we met one another even four years ago.

Just a date.

Resigned, yet excited at the same time, I took a deep breath and shot him a coy smile over my shoulder. "You got time tonight, Greyson Stone?"

STONE

Twelve months I spent trying to work down this girl, and it was fucking worth the wait.

For the sake of her brothers, we took separate vehicles back to my place, where she hopped into my Jeep and we spent an hour driving up and down the coast.

It was fun.

It was light.

We laughed and joked, talking about nothing important but, for whatever reason, that felt important.

"We're near my place, if you want to go there? We can order something?" she asked, looking at me from her spot in the passenger seat.

The roof was off and her black pony tail was blowing every which way around her face. She reached up to grab the end, holding it to her shoulder as she waited for my answer.

I was a healthy twenty-six year old man. I would be lying if I didn't say I was hopeful that going back to her place meant more than just eating.

But I also realized Brenna kept me at arm's length for the past year, and there was likely a reason other than her brothers. She never talked about dates or guys or, hell, anything, in her past.

Recalling the timidity in her eyes when we first met, I was willing to bet there was a story there.

I wasn't going to push though.

"Sure, we can do that."

I turned the music down slightly so it could still be heard over the roaring of the passing road and cars, but also so I could hear Brenna's directions.

During a straight shot, Brenna sat up straight in her chair, a huge smile on her beautiful face. "I love this song!" She reached for the dial and turned up the volume. It was Old Dominion's "Song for Another Time."

As she began to sing with the words, I chuckled to myself. This was my favorite CD at the moment. When the song finished, the CD shuffled to my current favorite song, namely because it felt real to what I was doing with Brenna right now.

Not knowing these words, Brenna sat back, listening to the words of "Til It's Over," nodding her head and swaying during some of the bigger instrumental points. Still, she was good about pointing me in the right direction and with awesome timing, the song ended just as I pulled into her duplex.

"Let me open the garage so you can park inside. You know. In case." She hopped out of the Jeep before I could say something, but I shrugged mentally. She was a little paranoid about her brothers finding out we went out for a little while, but I'd let her have it. For now.

If this was going to continue, there was no way in hell I was keeping her a secret.

She was the type of girl you showed off. Not just because she was beautiful, but because she was fun. She was sun and laughter all wrapped into a pretty package.

When the garage door lifted, I pulled the Jeep in, shutting off the ignition and climbing out just as she hit the button to close the door again.

Following her into her place, I looked around at the largeness. It was open and had a staircase that led to a lofted area. "You live here by yourself?"

She nodded. "Yeah. I shared it with a roommate up until a few months ago but she moved out and it's all mine now. Rent's not terrible for being in this area."

The garage door led right into the kitchen and dining area, which looked fairly updated with the slate floors and nice counters. Even the cabinets looked to be more modern than I would have thought for a duplex in this area.

"It's really nice."

She nodded. "Yeah. It was one of Rory's projects a few years ago. Well, not the actual renovation, but the planning of it. After, it was what gave Conor the inspiration to completely reno the pub."

I walked around the space slowly, taking everything in. If the kitchen and dining were the back half of the house, with a door leading to what I could only guess were the laundry room and a bathroom, the front half was the living area. The floors there were a natural wood and her furniture was incredibly nice too.

Shit, did these people have money and I didn't know it?

I stuffed my hands in my back pockets and turned back toward her, putting a smile on my face. So she had nice digs and a nicer place to sit down at night. But knowing what I did about Brenna, little as it may be, I didn't think that any of this was for show.

"Food?"

Brenna gave me her full, real smile, the one that brought out a dimple parallel to the bottom of her left eye, and nodded. "Sure. What would you like? I have pizza on autodial."

And that was what we ate for our first meal.

Nothing terribly special.

Nowhere fancy.

But comfortable, and cozy, and enjoyable.

After the pizza was eaten and everything put away, Brenna and I sat on her overstuffed leather couch in absolute silence. She lost her heels right after the pizza arrived.

She wore heels every shift. Sometimes I wondered if it were just her being stubborn, trying to prove a point after our first conversation about them. Still, I never caught her grimacing or even toeing them off during her breaks. She wore them like she was born in them.

If she were turned, I'd probably offer her a foot rub. I could only imagine her moan of pleasure as I dug my thumbs into her arches.

But I was rather comfortable right here, right now, with her curled into my side.

I noticed she didn't have a television, but I didn't want the obtrusion anyway. At some point, Brenna grew more comfortable with me and was now curled up into my side, her head on my shoulder and my arm around her. Her fingers traced lazy circles on my denim covered thigh but every now and then, her hand would pause and I would feel her tremble.

For all of her laughter and smiles, I got the sudden feeling that maybe her holding me back had a shit-ton to do with her, rather than her brothers.

"Dance with me?" I asked, picking up her hand in mine.

She sat up and smiled slightly. "Sure?" Her brows drew in for a moment, making me chuckle.

"Don't worry about the music, Angel."

If anything, that made her frown deepen, but still she rose from the couch when I pulled her to stand, willingly moving into my body when I brought her closer.

With both of her small hands in one of mine I brought her closer, my other hand to the small of her back. She was pressed against me everywhere and I fucking loved it. She was a little stiff, but my guess would be she simply felt awkward. Hell, there was no music—it *was* slightly awkward.

But I brought my A-game tonight.

I was no Justin Timberlake, but I could sing when needed.

With my voice low and soft, I sang to her, our bodies rocking slightly back and forth in the light of her living room. I sang to her a classic Sinatra song, and led that into "Till It's Over," my version a little more sensual and slower than the version she swayed to in the Jeep earlier. When I got to the 'naked making out' part though, Brenna pulled back laughing.

It was the most alive I had seen her face in the short time I'd known her. "They don't say that!" Her eyes were bright, her smile wide, but she didn't pull her hands from the cage mine put them in.

I grinned crookedly. "But they do. You've interrupted my song." My hand on her lower back rubbed in small circles. "*...or keep our clothes on. Don't—*"

"But those aren't the words. It's 'makin' makin' out.'"

I barked out a laugh, my own smile growing wide. "This isn't Chitty Chitty Bang Bang, Brenna."

"Seriously though? 'Naked makin' out?'"

Reluctantly, I let go of her hands to pull my phone from my pocket. I was more than pleased when she kept her hands on my chest, spreading her fingers over me. I kept my hand on her back though, not wanting to let go of any more points of contact. Quickly, I pulled up a search result for the lyrics to the Old Dominion song and double-tapped the screen, zooming in on the first verse.

With my thumb under the words, I showed her the phone. "See? Naked makin' out."

She spoke through her wide smile, shaking her head. "That's ridiculous."

I tossed my phone toward the couch, kind of thankful it actually landed on the couch and not the hardwood floor, and wrapped my arm around her shoulders, pulling her impossibly close. Lowering my head toward her ear, I swayed us back and forth to the music in my head. "But it's true," I whispered to her.

She burrowed into me, slipping her arms around my waist, and swayed with me as I sang her the rest of the song.

CHAPTER THREE

BRENNA

Stone scared me.

Things I felt around him were things I hadn't felt before, not in my teenaged years, nor my twentieth year, of surrounding myself with guys.

Much like the words he sang to me, he didn't try anything more than to sway with me in my living room. The feel of his hard body pressed against mine had my heart fluttering like mad. Add to that the fact that he was clearly aroused yet tried *nothing*…

My goodness, this man.

Eventually, he grabbed his phone and turned on a Spotify station and I found I missed his low, raspy singing voice, the grit in his words, his voice in my ear. But having music to sway to helped to keep the moment light.

After what had to be the tenth song, I leaned back from his arms and searched his face. What I was looking for, I wasn't entirely sure.

His gray eyes bore down into mine, but he said nothing, did nothing. Not that I did either. We stood and stared at one another for a few long moments and rather than feel awkward it felt…

Freeing.

Stone was unlike any man I had been around and while, like I said, it scared me, it also had me excited and curious. What would it be like to be in this man's arms in the primal sense?

I dropped my eyes to my hands, spread on his broad chest. With a deep breath, I found the courage to fully break my clause, putting my trust in this man I didn't fully know but who made me feel like something, someone, I hadn't felt ever before.

Moving my green gaze back to his gray one, I slid my hands up his chest, brushing along the sides of his thick neck, and placed them gently on his scruffy cheeks. Still, my eyes searched his, this time looking for a reason to stop, a reason to step back into my safe walls.

There weren't any.

I pushed up on tiptoe, gently pulling his face down to meet me. His eyes never left mine.

Before I could press my lips to his though, he spoke. "We don't have to, Bren."

So I whispered against his, "But I want to."

His lips pressed to mine, not giving me the chance to close the small gap myself. His hands moved from my back down to my ass and before I could prepare myself, he lifted me up. I gasped into his mouth which only served as an opening for him to sweep his tongue into mine.

The feel of the thickness in my mouth had me moaning. I moved a hand to the back of his blond head, wrapping my other arm around his neck. Between my arm and my legs wrapping around his hips, I was entwined around him like a monkey, I was sure, but I gave two fucks. My body was pulsing, my core was wet, and I wanted nothing more than to be completely engulfed by this man.

"Upstairs," I whispered against his mouth.

I felt him pause and knew without a doubt that this man here was a good man. He was considering what I was telling him.

But I gave him permission already. I wanted him, us, upstairs.

Finally, he moved us toward the stairs without further direction and excitement coursed through my body. He kissed me until we were about halfway up the steps, where he stumbled.

I laughed as he mumbled, taking the rest of the stairs with his mouth away from mine.

I wanted to pull his lips back to mine when he reached the landing, but he moved us directly to the bed. With me still wrapped around him, he moved onto the bed, knees first, moving to the middle and lowering us.

We probably made out, fully clothed, on that bed for an hour. It was the most delicious hour I had ever spent with someone's hands roaming over my body, under my clothes, as we learned one another.

When our clothes finally made their way to the floor, Stone stopped me from trying to climb over him again, instead pushing me back and laying his mouth to my pussy before I could stop him.

With one long sweep of his tongue, I was nearly in ecstasy.

I ground myself against his mouth as his tongue and lips worked magic over my clit. When he thrust his tongue into me, I had to grip the sheets at my sides. I was so incredibly close to coming.

Again, his mouth was at my clit and he hummed against me, bringing a whole new set of feelings down there. I clenched down on my muscles to try and stop my impending orgasm. I closed my eyes, focusing on his mouth on me, and I felt as he trailed a finger over my pussy lips, feather light.

Goodness, I was going to come so hard.

The softness of his finger and the magic of his mouth had me fighting toward a high I'd never reached before. All it would take was one bite, one thrust, and there wasn't going to be any way I could stop myself from

jumping over the edge.

And sure enough, when Stone slowly, so freaking slowly, pushed his thick finger into me, I shattered around him. "Stone!"

STONE

Her body bowed in ecstasy was a sight I couldn't have imagined. Her responses were better than I could have thought up.

My middle finger wasn't even completely buried in her and she was pulsing around me, her back arched and body tight. Keeping my finger in her, I moved up so I could kiss her, needing my mouth on hers. Her body relaxed slightly but her breathing was still heavy as I locked my mouth over hers. Her hands went in my hair and her tongue met mine, thrust for thrust. When I felt her wet channel slow down, I began to thrust my finger in and out of her, slowly, mimicking what I so badly wanted to do with my cock. I bent my finger, just enough so I could explore her walls, all while kissing and swallowing her moans.

Her hips shifted under us, her legs spreading as she fought to find another release.

Good fucking lord, I could love on her all night.

I added another finger to the mix, moving slowly again to get her used to the added width. She was tight and slick and I just fucking *knew* I was going to have a hard time holding my shit back when I finally sank into her.

"Stone," she moaned, pulling away from my mouth.

I had been Stone to everyone for a long fucking time—to family and friends alike—but for the first time since I left my first name behind in high school, I wanted someone to call me by my given name. I kissed her cheek, allowed my lower teeth to scrape over her as I moved my mouth toward her ear. "Grey."

She didn't ask for me to elaborate, she didn't question it. No, instead she turned her head toward mine and locked eyes with me. "I need you, Grey."

If that wasn't a boost for the ego…

Her using my name was like my own type of Kryptonite. Her husky, sex-heavy voice saying my name had my spine tingling but I'd be damned if I was blowing this soon.

I leaned back on my haunches and, after reaching for my pants on the ground and fishing out a condom, grabbed my hard girth and covered myself. I lowered the head to notch right where I wanted to be, where she wanted me to be.

Needing a moment to fully appreciate everything, I slid the tip up her wet folds, gathering moisture, before positioning myself once again, pushing into her slowly as I lowered my body to hers again.

I was going to love on her slowly this first time.

And then I was taking her every which way until the morning light.

I kept my thrusts slow, cocking my hips up every time I sank fully home. Every time I dragged out, Brenna bit on her lip. Every time I pushed all the way to the brink, she closed her eyes and moaned. She was going to end up with a sore lip, so rather than let that happen, I dropped my mouth to hers, kissing her slowly and in time with my thrusts.

There came a point though that I needed more. I could feel my orgasm coming again and I needed her closer to her own peak. Holding her body closer still, I quickened my pace, my open mouth breathing roughly against her ear, hers doing the same. Little mewling moans broke through her gasps and fuck if I didn't love them.

I reached between us, finding her clit with my thumb, rubbing circles over the nub as I pushed myself in and out. "Come on, Brenna. Let go, Bren," I told her, kissing her cheek.

Her breath hitched once, twice, and finally her jaw dropped open and her body bore down as her orgasm took her. I held myself in her deep, kissing her eyelids, her nose, and finally her mouth, as I waited for her body to calm before I continued, needing to find my own release. Holding myself deep in her, feeling her pulsing, squeezing against my hard cock and *not* coming right along with her should have won me a Goddamn medal.

When her body stopped moving, she opened her eyes and smiled up at me.

"You ready for more?" I asked her. When she nodded, I sat up to kneel between her legs, never dislodging my cock from it's warm, wet home. I slowly started to grind my lips, allowing the drag to be slow before I grabbed her behind the knee, holding one of her legs up. She put her foot on my shoulder and with a hand on her hip and the other on her knee, I began a ruthless rhythm. I watched her tits bounce with each thrust for a bit before she covered them with her hands, only to pluck at her nipple.

Her slick channel was growing wetter and she was moaning again, her fingers playing herself expertly and my cock driving into her again and again.

"God, Bren, I'm gonna..." I grunted, trying to hold back a few moments longer. I didn't want to leave her; I didn't want to end the feeling of her enveloping me. Goddamn, this was close to the best sex of my life and I didn't want it to end. "Fuck, I can't..." With a shout, I thrust into her once more, harder than before, my body shuddering as my own orgasm overtook me.

I didn't think she'd have it in her, but Brenna's body was taut under me again, her fingers pinched tight over her nipples and her eye squeezed shut in ecstasy. I could feel her squeezing against my cock as it fought to rid itself of cum.

Hands down, best sex of my life.

Three more rounds later and it was nearly four in the morning. The hours just flew by, between rounds of sex and quick catnaps.

Brenna lay against me and my fingers traced over the swirls and lines covering her back.

They surprised me when I took her from behind. It wasn't a tattoo I would have imagined for a girl like Brenna.

It was a huge piece, taking up her entire back. Rather than angel wings or butterfly wings, it was an abstract line piece of a whole butterfly.

"What's your tattoo mean?" I asked. Someone like Bren wouldn't get a huge-assed tattoo for no reason. An infinity somewhere, sure; peer pressure and all that, but this was a serious piece.

Brenna froze against me as if I'd said something that upset her. I lowered my chin to look down at her, trying to gauge her reaction, but she just gave me a tight smile.

"It's just pretty," she finally answered.

I honestly didn't think that was the full answer, but I'd let her leave it at that for now. Her hand had found its way to my cock and I wanted nothing more than to go through another round with this woman right here.

Serious questions and serious answers could wait.

CHAPTER FOUR

ONE YEAR AGO

STONE

"That's the last of my shit," I said after depositing a box in the bedroom Brenna and I would now be sharing officially.

My girl sat on the bed, grinning that wide, beautiful smile of hers, the one that made her green eyes dance.

The one that had me wanting to strip her of her clothing and love on her all night long.

We were good with the all-nighters. I suppose it helped that we were both night owls, but there was nothing I liked more than laying in her bed, waiting for her to come back to me, when I knew I was going to get sweet loving for hours on end.

Or even vice versa, knowing that I was going back to her place where she'd be waiting for me.

But now her place, her huge lofted duplex, was now our place.

We still hadn't told her brothers, which definitely didn't sit well with me. Brenna and I had been seeing one another, dancing around this, for *three damn years*. It was fucking difficult to keep on the down-low. I wanted to shout on the rooftops that I was in love with this girl, but I had to keep it to myself.

Well, and to Brenna. As far as I knew, she didn't know that I loved her; I hadn't told her yet. I was afraid that the words would send her running for the hills.

For three years, we went on occasional dates and had a number of secret sleepovers, either at her place or mine. We even went on vacations twice a year, she and I.

Brenna always had to come up with our excuses though, so her brothers wouldn't catch on. I had waited until I was completely moved in to her place before asking her about it though. Now was that time.

I knew my question was going to take the smile from her face, so I decided to kiss on her first, needing her full, open happiness for a moment longer.

I stalked toward her, loving the giggle she gave as she scrambled back to the middle of the bed. She was such an open and free spirit when it was just she and I. I wished, for her, that she would let go of the things that weighed her down. I knew a little about her past but I had a feeling that it only grazed the surface, that there was more to it than being the sheltered, over-protected sister of Conor and Rory O'Gallagher.

I crawled over her, grinning down at her. "You happy, Brenna O'Gallagher?"

Her smile grew smaller, but the joy was still written all over her face. She hooked her hand around my neck. "Absolutely, Greyson Stone."

"So," I said, finally broaching the subject of her brothers as she and I lay in bed, just a sheet draped over us after another marathon hour of sex. "I'm going to have to update my address on file."

Here's the thing.

Brenna was fucking smart. She had a degree in Business Management and was working on her Masters in the same field, yet, for whatever reason, hadn't told her brothers that either. When I brought it up to her, back when she first started the online program, she simply shook her head, saying that she wasn't ready for her brothers to know. I let it sit at that, but it was yet another thing about this woman that I didn't understand.

She was bright as the fucking sun. As beautiful as the sun setting over the beach.

But she kept so much about herself back from her brothers and I didn't understand why.

She told me once that if I wanted to be with her, I was going to have to be ok with her walls and because I *did* want to be with her, I overlooked them.

Didn't mean it didn't kill me a little inside, though.

I figured that my statement would have her realizing that we were going to have to tell her brothers about us, but no, her brilliant mind came up with a different alternative that I didn't see coming.

"Then just tell Con you want to pick up your statements. He'll be happy to save the pub forty-odd cents," Brenna said with a shrug.

I sighed but covered it up with a kiss to her forehead. "Bren," I said against her forehead. "How do you see this working? Us living together and them not finding out eventually?"

"Time, Grey." She looked up into my eyes. "I just need a little more time."

I thought three years was plenty of time, but what was a few more days?

CHAPTER FIVE

BRENNA

With Grey working today but being off myself, I found myself at the mall.

Just as I was leaving to head home though, I was nearly plowed down by a pregnant woman.

Ok, so plowed down may be a little overzealous. I wasn't paying attention, she wasn't paying attention, and then BAM! I ran into her. Or she me.

But when I looked into the woman's shocked face, I knew without a doubt, mine mirrored hers.

"Mia Hampton?"

Mia had been my best friend growing up. She and I had been thick as thieves, getting into mischief and taunting my older brothers relentlessly. We stopped being friends when we were ten though, but while we hadn't hung out, I still saw her now and then throughout the halls in school.

But this was the first time I'd seen her since graduation.

When we were younger, people would sometimes make the rude comment about how much of a pretty girl I was and how *not* pretty Mia was. Heck, my brothers even had some not very nice names for her, but looking at her now? Mia grew into herself extremely well.

Gone was the insecure, thicker girl and in her place was a gorgeous woman.

She gave me a timid smile. "Hey, Brenna."

"Oh my God, it is you! You look fantastic!" I knew that probably wouldn't go over well. One of those true rumors from my past was that I pushed Mia aside because she was the fat half of our friendship. I knew that was a rumor she knew too well.

Her smile lifted a little. "Thank you. You do too."

"God I love your curls." I reached out mindlessly to pull one of them, allowing it to bounce. "Remember when we were kids and we got a lock stuck in a fan?"

Her smile filled into a laugh. "My mother wasn't too happy about that. The bowl cut doesn't work too well with this hair."

I laughed too, remembering the time when we were eight and life was carefree, easy... There weren't worries about popularity or boys, or who you hung out with.

After a moment though, I recalled the fact that she was pregnant.

Very pregnant.

"Oh my goodness, look at your baby bump! You're so freaking cute, Mia. Where's your husband?" I peered around her, sure that whoever was with her wouldn't let her stay away for long.

Her smile fell this time and she shook her head. "I'm not married."

My brows rose a fraction. Mia was single and pregnant? Not that that was an atrocity in our world these days, but it simply wasn't something that fit in with the person Mia had been.

"The baby was an accident." While a seemingly negative comment, Mia said it with a small smile. "But a good one." She rubbed her swollen tummy.

I had so many questions for her, but standing outside of a maternity store wasn't the place to have them. "Do you want to go get coffee or something? I mean, decaf for you."

She stared at me for a moment, her eyes searching mine, before she

finally nodded. "Ok. Sure."

CHAPTER SIX

BRENNA

What a whirlwind of thirty-six hours.

After Mia confessed just *who* her "baby daddy" was, I concocted a plan to get her and Conor back in the same place. Sure, it was at my birthday dinner, but I wanted them face to face once again.

Sure, I wanted Conor to own up to what he'd done, but more so, I wanted Mia to tell Conor. Conor deserved to know, but I also couldn't help but want to see my oldest brother with my once best friend. It didn't surprise me that Mia had liked Conor once upon a time, and I was willing to bet there was still a small part of her that wanted to see if she could like him now.

The only problem with all of this though, was the blow-up that happened after the re-meeting.

I hadn't thought there would be anger and pinched faces. I should have figured, knowing Conor's personality, but I really honestly hadn't thought it would get to the point it did. Just when I thought I could potentially find a friend—again—in Mia, I went and screwed that up.

Watching Mia cry, watching as she pointedly glared at me, had the past all rushing back to me. Back to when I pushed her away. Back to when I started making stupid decisions.

Back to when I started to close off who I really was from the world.

It was time to start letting that out.

But there was only one person I wanted to talk to.

Even if the conversation would kill me.

STONE

When I got home from the pub, I was surprised to see Brenna's car in the garage. It was early yet for her to be done with dinner with her brothers.

"Hey, Bren, what's up?" I asked, walking into the living room where she sat on the couch, her legs folded under her. I dropped my keys and wallet on the kitchen table, moving toward her.

"I want to talk to you." Her voice was void of emotion, but her eyes were sad.

Shit, what the hell did I do?

I may be annoyed with the keeping things secret thing, but damned if I wanted this to end now.

"Ok, yeah. Sure." I moved to sit on the loveseat adjacent to the couch Brenna occupied and my racing heart calmed a fraction when she unfolded herself to sit next to me on the much smaller couch.

I angled myself in the corner so I could face her and Brenna sat completely sideways, her legs under her once again, and her head resting on the back of the couch.

"So I invited Mia to dinner tonight."

"Mia, as in the girl you ran into at the mall?" Yesterday, Brenna explained to me, in excitement, about this meeting of her once best friend. That excitement wasn't anywhere on her face now though.

"Yeah, but she's a little more than just a once-friend." Brenna took a shaky breath and I was hit with the knowledge that this was it.

No, not as in the end of our relationship, but as in she was going to

completely open up to me. I was going to learn about her walls.

"I know I told you Mia was once my best friend and that we sort of fell apart, but that was only a half-truth." Her hands were folded in her lap and she looked down, her raven hair blocking her face from me.

I didn't want her hiding herself from me, so I reached out and pushed her hair back behind her ear. She may not give me her eyes right now, but I could at least see her face to a degree.

"When I was ten, I decided Mia was too...different from me to stay my friend." Her words were choked. I could feel the disappointment in herself, behind her words. She was ashamed of herself and that had me frowning.

I reached for her chin to lift her face toward mine. "You were ten. It happens."

Brenna shook her head and pulled back from my hand, her eyes sadder than I had ever seen them before.

And she had me sitting through some pretty gut-wrenching movies in our time together.

"No. It was incredibly mean of me. She was fat and I wasn't, and the cool kids wouldn't talk to me with her hanging around. So I pushed her away. I pushed her away so I could hang with the cool kids." She took another one of those shaking breaths, her hands fisted so tightly together that her knuckles were pale. I reached for her hands and gently pried them apart, allowing her time to speak when she was ready.

"Well, the cool kids have a way of biting you in the ass and not giving a shit," she said around a sad smirk. "I started smoking when I was twelve. I stopped, but it happened. I had more boyfriends than I could count by the time I was fourteen."

The more she refused to meet my eyes, the more I realized I didn't want this truth any more. I didn't want to watch her break herself open.

"Brenna." I tugged her close, glad when she willingly crawled into my lap. "It doesn't matter. None of it matters, Angel." I rubbed my hand up and down her back but she shook her head against my chest.

With her face buried into my shoulder, her body shaking, she gave me a truth I would have never guessed. "My tattoo isn't because it's pretty. It's in memory of the baby I lost."

CHAPTER SEVEN

BRENNA

His hand froze on my back.

I knew it.

I just *knew* that if he knew the truth, he'd likely pull away.

I swallowed, begging in my mind for him to keep holding me a moment longer, to not let me go for just a little while longer.

I chose butterfly wings for the little girl that I named Nova. I didn't have a lick of Native American in me, but the name meant 'chasing butterflies' and that's what I wanted for the baby who wouldn't ever see a birthday. I wanted to imagine her somewhere bright and happy, chasing butterflies and being a regular, beautiful little girl.

"Ok," Grey broke into my thoughts.

That was it. Just 'ok.'

I pulled my head away from him to frown up at his face, surprised to see it wasn't contorted in disbelief or disgust, but rather…concern?

"So are you sad today because you ran into an old friend who's pregnant? Or because of something else?" His question only held curiosity and had me pausing before answering him. When I still hadn't, he started rubbing small circles over my back again.

I searched his eyes, but had a feeling I wasn't going to find what I was looking for. I wasn't going to find judgement from his man. Not once in the four years knowing him had I seen him being judgmental about anyone.

"Do you want to talk about it?" he asked instead.

Not really but, "I was seventeen. I couldn't tell you who the father was." I burrowed back into Grey's chest, not wanting to have this conversation but knowing that because I started it, he deserved to hear the rest.

To learn why I needed to keep things from my brothers.

"My brothers thought I was some freaking angel, but really I was spreading my legs for any guy who smiled at me. Heck, they didn't even have to smile." My voice caught in my throat when Grey's hand stopped yet again but rather than push me away, he hugged me tight.

It was his silence that urged me to go on.

"I lost her at twenty-two weeks. A spontaneous late miscarriage," I whispered. "It was winter, so I could hide my belly behind baggy sweatshirts and no one thought anything of it. Well, except the kids at school. Someone found out I'd been pregnant and it was all over the school in the matter of a day. When I never showed, it didn't stop the rumors from circling but every time I heard it, it crushed me.

"I wasn't ready to be a mom, but I felt that me losing my baby so late was God's way of punishing me. Or karma. Really bad karma." I squeezed my eyes shut, picturing the day I had to deliver her. The day I delivered my dead baby, all by myself, not a single person who mattered to me, standing beside me. "I delivered her and held her. She was so tiny, but so, so perfect." My breath hitched again. "Her tiny nose, her hands. She wasn't any bigger than my hands but, in that moment, I knew what it was to love and lose, and I hated it."

I took a deep breath and pushed back from my spot, wiping at my eyes with the palms of my hands before staring into Grey's eyes yet again, still on his lap for as long as he'd let me stay.

"I got over the hurt by sleeping around more. When I was nineteen, I realized I didn't like the girl in the mirror, so I stopped. I vowed to not allow myself to be that girl ever again, to not find comfort in a set of arms."

Grey nodded, reaching out and wiping at my tears with his thumbs. "And your brothers don't know." He said it with such quiet calm.

I shook my head. "No. They don't know who I was in those

years. And they never questioned that I stopped dating, that I never brought guys around."

"I think you should tell them," he said, still without a drop of judgment on his face, only concern, as he looked into my eyes.

Still though, I shook my head. "No. I don't want them to know. Ever."

I was thankful when Grey let that sit. The mood was incredibly somber but I was grateful he hadn't put me aside and left me here to deal with these emotions alone.

"What made you break your vow?" he asked, sometime later.

I could finally smile. "You. Just you."

CHAPTER EIGHT

BRENNA

It had been nearly a year since Grey moved in, a year since he learned my most heartbreaking secrets, but still our relationship was strong.

In that time, Conor became a daddy for the first time. Aiden Rory O'Gallagher was the cutest little button with his daddy's hair and eyes. Watching as Conor went from playboy to loving boyfriend, even further to doting dad, was one of the best transformations I had the pleasure of watching.

In that time, Mia and I grew incredibly close again. I shared with her some of my past secrets, keeping the biggest ones to myself. The night I confessed them to Grey was one of the worst nights I'd ever experienced. More than once, I woke up in a cold sweat, crying from dreams I couldn't remember, but could only imagine they dealt with Nova. Grey simply held me tight, kissing away my tears, and loving me back into oblivion.

While our schedules were all over the place, we never missed an opportunity to be in one another's arms, a place I found I loved more than anything. The way Grey made love to me, owning my body and driving my needs to completion, had me falling for him in ways that scared me. And because of that, I started worrying that someday this wouldn't be enough for Grey.

But, right now, it seemed like it was plenty for him.

He had me pressed against the counter, a hand kneading my breast over my shirt and bra, and his mouth on my neck, nibbling in ways that had goosebumps trailing up and down my body.

"Grey, my brothers are coming!" I said, trying to push him away from me. One of us had to be the levelheaded one. "You have to go."

He groaned but pulled away. I shivered at the loss of his warm mouth on my skin, even though the distance was what I needed right now.

"Jesus, Bren," he said. I knew he was annoyed with this part of the situation. He started talking about bringing us up to my brothers about a month ago. "Can't we just tell them yet?"

I shook my head.

No.

My brothers liked Grey and if they found out he'd been sleeping with me, let alone living with me for the last year, they would surely blow a fuse. Both of them.

"We have to put your stuff away," I said, my mind in frantic mode as I looked around the duplex for any signs of Grey.

He was all over.

He lived here; of course, he was all over.

I stuffed things in the cubes under the coffee table, more things in the hall closet, knowing my brothers wouldn't go in there. I barely noticed when Grey shook his head and headed to the kitchen.

Hopefully to remove any evidence he lived here in there too.

I ran down the hall to be sure all of our clothes were put away, then into the bathroom to move his products into the linen closet.

When I moved back into the living area, fifteen minutes before my brothers were to arrive, Grey was standing by the front door, his shoes on and shrugging into a jacket.

"I hate this, Bren."

"It's only for a little while longer," I lied. I wasn't sure when I would be comfortable telling my brothers.

And as much as I trusted Grey, cared for him, there was still a small piece of me that was terrified of what would happen to me when he decided he'd had enough of me.

When he decided to walk away.

At least whenever that happened, if my brothers didn't know about us, he could go on living his life the way he had been.

"I want to tell them."

My eyes flew to his. "Please don't. Not right now."

"Brenna, they deserve to know everything you've gone through."

A mind of their own, my hands covered my flat stomach and I shook my head. "No."

He stared at me a little longer before shaking his head sadly. Without a word, he turned and left the duplex.

I took a deep breath, trying to calm the racing of my heart.

However, the racing came from a whole different type of anxiety than my brothers finding out.

No, the racing was because suddenly I was very afraid of losing Greyson Stone.

"Isn't that Stone's?" Conor asked as he walked into the kitchen, pulling out a chair at my tiny table. He sat down with Aiden in his lap. I followed his eyes and saw what his had landed on.

Sure enough, Grey's hoodie was in the corner, where he had thrown it off me earlier.

"Um." I looked around frantically. "I borrowed it last night." I refrained from nodding and looking like a crazed person. "When I left the pub, it was chillier than I anticipated and he let me wear it home."

Thankfully, that answer seemed to appease my brothers, as the subject dropped and changed to the upcoming get-together we were planning for our parents' return to San Diego.

Rory decided he wanted to order pizza, and the two of them stayed longer than I thought they would. By the time they left, Aiden had been napping on the living room floor for an hour.

I sent a text Grey, letting him know it was safe to come back home, but when he didn't answer—when I went to bed alone— that earlier anxiety of losing Grey came rushing back.

CHAPTER NINE

STONE

Angel: They're gone. You can come home now.

I stared at my phone, wanting above everything to just tell her off. I was sick of this.

Five years.

Five years I've known Brenna and have essentially been doing just this. Sure, it was ok at first, but shortly after moving in with her, things started to take a much, much more serious turn for me.

Five years was a long time to be with someone.

And it was mentally longer when you had to do it in secret.

I didn't want to date her in secret any more.

What was I going to do, marry her in secret? Send her away on year-long vacations so she could have babies in secret?

Because that's where my mind, my fucking heart, was right now.

I didn't play along with this game for five years just to say goodbye to her, no. I played along because I knew she was it for me.

The four hours that I wasn't allowed in my own fucking place, I mindlessly drove around the Bay. I spent a good amount of time at La Jolla, sitting and watching the seals sunbathe.

I still hadn't answered Brenna's text when the sun started to sink over the horizon but she hadn't tried to get back to me, either.

I stood from my perch on a rock and headed back to my car, squeezing the bridge of my nose.

Knowing Brenna, she was probably mentally preparing for me to say goodbye to her. Whenever she revealed a piece of her past, it was like she curled herself into a coat of armor, waiting for me to decide I was done.

As if her past did anything other than make me love her more.

Did I hate that she kept her life so far apart from her brothers? Yes.

But I admired her for the things she shouldered, for the things she went through—alone.

The fact that I waited so long to respond now—well, to *not* respond—probably had her head in some insecure headspace.

God, I loved her so much and I physically ached for her and the pain she went through by herself for so many years. I wanted her to open up and tell her brothers. I wanted her to take that weight off her own chest.

She had nothing to be ashamed of.

Me: *I'm on my way home*

I pocketed my phone before I could talk myself into waiting for her response.

BRENNA

I was already in bed by the time Grey came home.

I didn't roll over, didn't greet him. I could feel his frustration the moment he cleared the loft stairs though.

Squeezing my eyes shut, I forced my body to relax. I could hear as he moved around the room, discarding his clothes before walking into the bathroom to brush his teeth and get ready for bed.

The lights clicked off in the bathroom and his footsteps fell softly on the carpet. I felt the bed dip behind me and I fully expected him to turn his back on me, to sleep apart from me.

I understood why he was upset.

It wasn't the first time he'd asked me to come clean to my brothers, about my past, about us.

But I was terrified.

Absolutely fucking terrified.

If my brothers knew what a slut I was growing up...

I couldn't bear to think of what their faces would look like.

And then, if they found out I'd been a pregnant teenager? Oh my God, Conor would probably be most pissed for that offense alone.

And like I thought earlier, if they knew about Grey and me...

Grey didn't deserve the wrath of Conor and Rory.

But what did that mean for Grey and me?

I was going to have to force him to bow out. I was going to have to convince him he didn't like me anymore, to get him to move out and away.

I stifled what would have been a sob. It ended up being more of a muted hiccup. I squeezed my eyes shut, hopeful Grey wouldn't notice.

The good thing with what Grey and I had been doing was that when he walked away, we could just continue going on like we had been in public. No one would know the difference.

He'd still flirt with everyone in a skirt, with a special brand for me, and I'd still give him eye-rolling hell.

And I could cry in private, because it was going to hurt to tell him goodbye.

Tomorrow.

I'd have to do it tomorrow.

I couldn't keep doing this.

I parted my lips to take a deep breath, releasing it shakily.

Resigned to my plans, I cuddled deeper into my pillow, willing the tears that threatened to stay at bay. It would do me no good to cry right now. I could do it tomorrow after Grey took his things and left.

But when he reached toward me, pulling me into his bare chest, I nearly lost my resolve. The tears that had been a mere threat before were now burning behind my closed lids, threatening to spill.

And when he pressed his lips to my shoulder, the words he spoke absolutely shattered my soul.

"I love you, Brenna."

CHAPTER TEN

STONE

When I crawled into bed with Bren last night, I knew she'd been awake, but she put on a good game.

I didn't know what was going through her head, but her slight trembles and shaky sighs fucking killed me. I knew right away I shouldn't have stayed away so long.

Fuck. I shouldn't have gone in the first place.

When I woke, Brenna was no longer in my arms. I looked around the room, not noticing any signs of her but seeing the door to the bathroom closed. Focusing, I could hear the shower running.

I didn't have to be in to the pub for a few hours, but Brenna had an early shift. I could get in the shower with her, save water and hopefully save whatever was crumbling in our relationship, but I had a feeling Brenna wouldn't be completely open to that at the moment.

With a resigned sigh, I rolled out of the bed and pulled on yesterday's jeans.

"Brenna, you're not listening to me." I'd been trying to get through to her since the moment she stepped out of the shower. When it was time for her to leave for the pub, I refused to end our talk at the standstill where it was currently at. She fought it, but eventually allowed me to drive her in to work.

Not that we got any further in our standstill.

"We aren't telling them, Stone!" She pushed out the Jeep's door and my heart tumbled not just her hasty retreat, but by her calling me Stone.

She never called me Stone when we weren't at the pub, putting on a disguise.

"Brenna, it's been five fucking *years*!" I slammed the door after I exited the Jeep.

"If it's too much for you, then you can take your things and leave." She stomped up to the front doors of O'Gallaghers, pushing through them.

I had to quicken my step to get to her before she got into the back. If she did, that was going to be the end of this conversation and, potentially, the end of us.

I wasn't about to let that happen.

I didn't date her in secret for damn near five years, living with her for one of those years, for this to all just go and disappear.

I did it because I thought that, at some point, she would change her mind and be open to telling her brothers. I didn't think it would take this long, in all honesty, and it was beginning to look like Brenna would have kept it like this until we ran our course.

But I didn't have plans on our relationship 'running its course.' Oh no. This course wasn't ending for another fifty or sixty plus years.

"Brenna. C'mon, Angel, let me talk to you." I took the steps two at a time and caught her hand, sliding in behind her before the door could close on me.

"We're not telling them!" Her voice was lowered but definitely full of heat.

"Why, Bren? Why." I pulled her into a darker area of the pub near the dart boards. I noticed Rory by the bar and as much as I'd like to tell him I was dating his sister—shit, living with her—I was going to let Brenna do it. Or let her give me permission to do it. But fuck if it was going to take more than today to get there.

"Because I'm not ready!"

"When will you be, Brenna? Seriously. It's been five fucking years. I *live* with you!"

"Then move out." She crossed her arms over her chest and while her words were defiant, there was a world of sadness in her eyes.

"That's a cop out, and you know it."

"They like you, Grey." Thank fuck she called me Grey. "If they found out what we've been doing, what we are doing, they're not going to like you anymore. You're going to be out a job, friends…" She shrugged a shoulder.

"Who the fuck cares, Brenna? It's *you* I want. Not the pub. Not your brothers. I would think that was made clear by the fact I've played this your way for this long. I also think you're not giving your brothers enough credit."

"Grey—"

"No. I'm not done. Do you need to tell them about your biggest mistakes growing up? No. Should you tell them the real meaning behind your tattoo? Yeah. Yeah, I think you should. Do I think they've put you in a bubble and are a little blind when it comes to you? Sure do. But that's on you just as much as it's on them. You are one of the strongest, *feistiest* women I know; you could have stepped out of that bubble at any time."

She shook her head again. "You don't understand."

"No, Bren, I don't think *you* understand. You've fallen into this victim's mentality when it comes to your past and I understand where your head's been, but you have support. You have your brothers—if you let them in. But you also have me.

"God, Brenna. I am so over the moon in love with you, but I can't keep doing this. I can't love you in secret and pretend nothing is going on during the day, not when all I want is to put a ring on your finger and a baby in your belly." I stepped back and put my hands in the air, resigned. "Can't do that in secret."

Again, Brenna shook her head. Or maybe she never stopped. "I can't right now, Grey." She looked defeated and while I hated I did that to her, I was glad I got my words out.

Now, to see how she would sit on those words. To see if she

would accept them or pack my shit for me, because I'd be damned if I was moving out on my own.

BRENNA

"Yo, Bren!" sounded from the other end of the bar. I looked away from Grey and his determined expression, toward the source of my name calling—Rory.

"What, Rory?" There was a bit of bite in my voice, but I was annoyed with the men in my life. Rory, for being his regular self, and currently Grey because he…

Well, because he loved me and that didn't fit in with the plan.

I pushed around Grey, needing the space but also needing to get ready for my shift.

"Leave the poor guy alone. What the hell did he do to you?"

I shook my head, mumbling to myself, "He just wants a little bit more from me than I'm ready for."

The earlier hours at the pub were surprisingly busy today and when Grey came on for his afternoon shift, I tried to avoid him. Well, as best as I could. We were working together for my last hour on the floor.

My thoughts last night about ending things with Grey, but everything being normal at work? Yeah, not sure how that was going to happen.

He refused to talk to me, other than when he and I had to deal with drink orders. He stayed on his end of the bar and I stayed on the floor. Every time I glanced over at him and saw him flashing his smile at a woman, my heart cracked a little.

This is what I wanted.

I wanted to push him away.

Thankfully, I didn't have to think about it too much longer. I slipped into the back room when my shift was up, grabbing my purse and phone. When I left the office, I nearly ran into Conor.

He grabbed my arm, steadying me from my bounce back.

"Hey, Bren. Mia wanted to know if you wanted to come for dinner."

I glanced toward the bar, then back toward Conor. I didn't have a ride home; I rode in with Grey. Besides, I needed a little bit of space.

"Yeah, sure."

When we got back to his and Mia's place, a squirming ten-month-old was thrust into my arms and my hair was pulled on, but the liveliness of the house had my spirits lifting.

I sat in the kitchen with Mia as she waddled around, her big baby belly getting in the way of everything. My heart swelled, watching my oldest brother put his hands on his very pregnant girlfriend's waist, putting her aside with a kiss on her temple, and telling her he'd finish getting dinner ready.

Conor fell into the domestic thing pretty quickly, but it fit him so well. He was a different guy these days than he was when he opened the pub. As much as Mia may have hated me when I threw the two of them together, forcing her to tell him who she was and that she was pregnant with this cutie pie sitting on my leg, I didn't regret a single moment of the piece I played in their getting together.

Mia, Aiden, and I moved to the living room where Mia sat on the couch and I on the floor with my nephew, rolling him a ball that he would promptly attempt to put in his mouth.

Aiden was all Conor. He had the same pitch-black hair that my brother and I shared, but also the startling blue eyes. He did have Mia's nose and chin, but there was absolutely no doubt who this kid's father was.

"Is Miss Ava getting ready to come out?" I asked, rolling the ball another time.

Mia groaned, putting her hand on the top of her large belly. "I sure hope so."

I laughed lightly and moved to my knees to crawl over to my nephew, scooping him up with one arm and moving back to sit. He giggled the entire time, his gummy, two-toothed smile wide and infectious.

God, I loved this baby and I knew without a doubt his baby sister was going to be just as lovely. I didn't envy Mia and her baby belly, no; I heard all too often how uncomfortable this pregnancy was making her, but the baby in my arms and the one who was due to make her appearance any day now?

They had flashes of blond haired, green-eyed babies in my head.

I never really thought about kids, not after losing Nova. Heck, even before I lost her, I never thought about kids. But being surrounded by babies and, damn him, Grey mentioning me having his babies...

The panicky feeling overcame my chest again, making it hard to breathe. I tried to keep it from Mia but the woman was incredibly perceptive.

"What's wrong, Bren?" She scooted to the edge of her seat and I didn't have a doubt in the world that if she could maneuver to the floor, and then get back up again, she'd be right next to me.

I shook my head, focusing on deep breaths. When I was sure I was going to be ok, I gave my friend a small smile. "Nothing. I'm fine."

Mia's eyes narrowed and I could tell she wanted to press, but thankfully, she let it be. "Alright well... I'm going to go check on Con. You good with Aiden?" With a hand on the couch beside her, she lifted herself to stand.

I fought to stop the grin from spreading on my face as I watched her. She was a fucking cute pregnant woman.

"We'll be fine." I turned Aiden so he faced me, having him stand on his chubby legs. "Won't we, boy-o?" He squealed his delight.

Once Mia left the room, I sighed and gave Aiden a small smile. "You're pretty cute, you know that?"

He bent his knees in a jump, and I allowed him to dip before pulling him back up to stand on my legs.

I glanced over my shoulder to be sure Con and Mia weren't within earshot. "What am I going to do about Grey?" I whispered to Aiden. He gave me a babbled answer. "Yeah, I know." Next, Aiden's hand went into his mouth. "You're tellin' me, buddy..."

I flipped him around so he sat in my lap, his back to my front, and reached for my phone. Regardless if I was putting distance between us, it would be rude of me not to let him know where I was. He was my ride to the pub and he'd likely expect me home tonight. I shot him a quick text that I was with Con and Mia, and that I'd be there for the night at the least, before turning my phone off. I didn't want to hear his response. Not yet.

CHAPTER ELEVEN

BRENNA

I avoided Grey another day.

But I had a good excuse; Mia was having contractions throughout the day, so she and Con asked if I could stick around to help with Aiden in case they had to leave. The day didn't bring a baby, but there was hope that the night would.

At around three in the morning, Conor tapped me on the shoulder, effectively rousing me from sleep.

"I'm bringing Mia to the hospital."

I sat up straight on the couch. "Now?" I frantically looked around. Mia was by the door, a pained smile on her face, and a bag by her feet.

"You're still good staying here with Aiden?" I nodded. "Absolutely. Yeah, sure."

Conor stood and pointed to the coffee table, where he put the video monitor. "He'll probably sleep for another three or four hours. I'll call you when it's go time. Mia's keys are on the hook; you can just take her car. Aiden's seat is already in it."

I smiled sleepily. God, this was exciting. I stood up and gave my brother a hug before moving to Mia, hugging her tight. "Go have a baby, Mia."

She laughed, hugging me back. "Thank you, Brenna." I could hear in her voice that her thank you was for more than just watching Aiden for the next few hours. I leaned back and gave her a smile.

"You are more than welcome, Mia."

"Someday you'll find your happy, and I can't wait to be there for you," Mia said, squeezing my shoulder. The squeeze got painfully tight as her face contorted.

"Shit, Mia, that's four minutes. We've gotta go."

Her face was still tight, her eyes shut, but she managed to hold up a finger for my brother. One second, she was saying.

I couldn't help but grin.

God, I loved these two.

Conor moved to grab their bag and wrapped an arm around Mia's back. "You let me know when you're good, Mia baby." I stepped away, giving them room, and after a moment longer, Mia nodded.

"Ok. Yeah. Let's go have this little lady." Mia smiled up at Con, who bent down to press a light kiss to her lips.

I had to look away.

What would it be like to have that?

Shit.

I'd had that.

And I, more or less, was throwing it away.

The anxiety in my chest was starting again, but I managed to hold it back until after I saw Conor's truck leave the drive.

God, what was I doing?

Five years ago, I met a man who made me feel things I hadn't in a long while before that point.

Four years ago, I took a chance and went on a date with that same man, a man who became a constant in my life.

Three years ago, one date turned to two, which turned into a once a week thing. We even threw a vacation or two in there.

Two years ago, we decided that the occasional date wasn't going to be enough, and we were at one or the other's place nearly every night.

One year ago, he and I decided life would be easier if he just moved in, like it was no big deal.

Cohabitation was completely normal. People did it all the time.

One day ago, I got scared because he told me he loved me.

So I pushed him away.

The only person in the world who knew all my secrets,

knew all my faults, yet still fucking loved me. He loved me, and I pushed him away.

When I looked at Aiden, I wanted something like him in the future.

When I looked at Conor and Mia, I was envious of their relationship.

But why?

I had what they had; I just refused to acknowledge it in person.

So what if my brothers decided he wasn't good enough for me, if they fired him and never looked at me again?

When did I get to start living my life, for me? When did I get to start loving my life, and let go of everything that held me back?

I moved back to the couch and picked up my phone from its spot next to the monitor. I looked at the monitor screen, making sure Aiden was still sleeping, before opening my text log.

It didn't surprise me that Grey never responded before. If there was one thing I was sure of, it was that I hurt him by walking away from his declaration.

If there was one thing he proved over the years, it was that he was willing to play things my way—but eventually he was going to stop playing.

Me: *Mia's off to have baby Ava.*

Not expecting a response—he closed and likely went to bed an hour ago—I turned off the screen and tried to settle back into sleep, knowing it likely wouldn't come.

I stared at the dark ceiling, my eyes tracking the slow moving fan as it whirled around in circles.

I didn't want to be alone. I didn't want the quiet.

I wanted laughter.

I wanted hugs, kisses, love, and I knew just who I wanted them from.

CHAPTER TWELVE

STONE

I couldn't sleep.

It had been a long fucking time since I went to bed alone, or without the knowledge that Brenna would be coming to bed, to me, in a matter of hours. And to do it two nights in a row didn't make it any better.

It fucking sucked.

I lay in bed, my arms back behind my head and the sheets down by my hips, my ears open and listening for her. Surely she would come home tonight.

She wanted me to pack up everything and leave?

No.

I wanted her to come home and fight it out with me. There had to be more to her reluctance to tell her brothers her past, other than simply she didn't want to ruin what they thought of her. To hell what they thought of me! I could give two fucks if they decided they didn't like me simply because I was in love with their sister.

I didn't think they'd be too pissed, anyway.

Not with Conor becoming Dad of the Year, and Rory doing...whatever the hell Rory was doing with Emily.

There was a story I couldn't wait to watch unfold.

I sighed heavily and tried closing my eyes, even though I knew sleep wouldn't come. I tried counting sheep, counting backward from one hundred, purposely relaxing every part of my body, starting down at my toes...anything that I had been told worked for someone somewhere.

But all with no such luck.

I let my eyes open again, staring at the white ceiling. Two sleepless nights were no joke.

When a Luke Bryan song started wafting through the duplex, I frowned momentarily. It was Brenna's ringtone for texting.

Shit.

It was Brenna's ring tone.

I jackknifed off the bed and moved to the other side of the loft, where we kept the charging dock for devices. I picked up my phone and ran my other hand through my hair, thumbing open the message.

Angel: *Mia's off to have baby Ava.*

I started a response and erased it probably five times before I just pressed call.

As the phone rang in my ear, I walked back to the bed, hoping against all hope that she would answer. *Please answer, Bren.*

Just when I thought it was going to go to voicemail, where I'd at least get to hear her voice, the call clicked on.

"Hey, Grey." Her voice was unsteady, unsure.

"Hi, Angel."

There was a moment where neither of us spoke and I could hear her breathing through the line.

"Do you want me to come over?" I asked finally.

She took a moment to respond. "You don't need to." She could be so stubborn. "Do you want me to come over?" I repeated.

"Yes."

It was whispered, but the single word packed a punch.

"Ok. Alright." I stood again and, holding the phone to my ear still, starting pulling out clothes to put on. "I can be there in ten minutes."

Ten minutes later, I pulled into the drive of Conor and Mia's house. I cut the engine and got up to the front door in record time. At three thirty in the morning, the little neighborhood was quiet, the only activity being maybe a plane flying overhead. Otherwise the night was silent, still.

I started to knock, not wanting to wake Aiden with the doorbell, but just as my knuckles hit the wood, the door was pulled open.

There she stood, in all her raven-haired beauty.

Her hair was loose and wavy around her shoulders. Add to that her bed attire of a tank and shorts, and her unsure face, and she looked tired in more ways than just from lack of sleep.

"Hey, Bren."

She stayed standing there, a hand on the door, staring up at me. I stayed put, waiting for her to tell me what had her pausing.

Finally, she said, "I'm sorry, Grey."

I shook my head. "You have nothing to be sorry about, Angel."

"No, I do," she said, shaking her own head. She stepped back, allowing me into her brother's home, and I took her hand in mine. I squeezed it once, and after the door was closed and locked, she led me to the living room.

We sat next to one another, her bare thigh pressed to my jean-clad one. I kept her hand in mine, not wanting to lose more contact.

"I'm ready to tell my brothers." She looked at me. "About us," she clarified.

I nodded. "Ok." I could take that. "Eventually, though…"

She shook her head, knowing where I was going. "They don't need to know, Grey."

I tugged her closer until she was sitting on my lap and I had my arms locked around her. "Their opinion of you is not going to change, Brenna. You are still their sister."

She dropped her eyes from mine, watching as she traced a finger down my chest. With her voice low, she said, "I don't want them to know. I don't want to open up that hurt again."

That I could understand. The night she told me about losing her baby, she definitely shattered in my arms. There were only so many times a person could do that and still find a way to put the pieces together again.

I took her chin in my fingers and lifted her face toward mine. "I do not judge you. You know this." I pecked her lips before finishing what I had to say. "If and when you decide to tell them, I *will* be there to help you pick up your pieces. You are strong, Angel. You can get through any of it."

She offered me a half smile which I gladly covered with my lips. We kept the kiss light and appropriate for our surroundings.

I wasn't about to make love to her in her brother's living room. Not happening.

"I love you, Brenna O'Gallagher," I said against her lips.

She pulled back this time, a hand on my face as she stared at me. She brushed her thumb over my lips, her eyes on the movement, before she shifted them back to mine. "I love you too, Greyson Stone."

My lips lifted on their own accord. "Yeah?"

"Yeah."

Before I could celebrate that news though, her phone chimed through the dark.

"Oh! It's probably Con," she said, scrambling off my lap. I took the moment to adjust myself, then stood to move toward her. "It's time. Oh good, it's time!"

"That wasn't long. We going?" I asked, unsure of what her plan had been.

She nodded, heading toward Aiden's room. "Yes. I just need to grab Aiden. Could you start the car? Mia's keys are on the hook."

I did as she asked, finding myself surprisingly excited to get to experience this with Brenna and her family.

BRENNA

Just as we parked, Conor texted to let me know that Ava Grace O'Gallagher made her entrance. With a sleeping Aiden in tow, Grey and I made our way to their room. I was excited to meet my little niece.

Grey held Aiden against his side and had my hand in the

other. I was anxious to walk into the room like this, I wasn't going to lie, but I was going to go through with it anyway.

"Congrats, Mama!" I said as we walked through the door, me leading my small pack.

"Thank you," Mia said from her perch on the bed, a smile on her face as she looked down at her bundle. But when her face lifted to us in the doorway, her eyes dropped to mine and Grey's linked hands, then back up to my face. Her own face dropped, her eyes wide and mouth open.

"Brenna O'Gallagher!"

Con, whose back was to us as we walked in, looked over his shoulder, frowning at Mia's outburst.

And then, to make the whole fiasco even more fun and exciting, Rory stepped into the room behind us.

"Guy uses the bathroom and comes back to squealing. What's going on?"

"Are you…?" Mia asked.

Grey's hand in mine tightened.

Support.

He was always giving me his support.

"Yes. We are," I answered.

Conor stood and Rory stepped around us to join him. Both had matching frowns on their faces.

It was funny how those two looked nearly nothing alike, but their expressions were mirror images.

"How long?" Conor asked, crossing his arms over his chest in that big, puffy way men sometimes got.

"Dude, they're holding hands. It's probably been awhile. Or else they'd have just walked in together." Rory, ever the thinker…

"We're not here to talk about Bren and me." Grey shifted Aiden in his arms, but the boy still slept.

"But let's!" Mia was giddy as all get out and I couldn't help but laugh lightly at her reaction. She should be tired after pushing out a baby but she was excited for me.

"And Bren's giggling. So maybe it's new. That's a new relationship sign."

I shook my head at Rory. He wasn't all that bright in the women department, which was probably why he had yet to secure Emily in his life.

I looked over to Grey only to see him looking at me. He was letting me decide how long. Because really...how long? Five years? That's when it started. One year? That's when it got seriously serious.

"Five years," I said, my chin rising.

"Five years?" Conor's face was contorted in confusion. "That was when—"

"Shit—" Rory started, but was interrupted by Mia yelling 'ears!', "You mean, every time I covered a shift for you, so you could go out with a girl, it was with my *sister*?"

"Seriously. Five years?" Conor couldn't seem to get past that.

"It was casual for the first few years, yeah, but I moved in last year," Grey offered, putting all our cards on the table.

Conor's eye swung to mine and where I semi-expected anger, there was just confusion. "Why the secrecy, Bren?"

I shrugged. "I wasn't ready."

And I left it at that. They could too.

"I'm so excited for you, Bren," Mia said. "Come here and look at your niece."

What she really meant was she and I were having a discussion apart from the boys.

Grey let go of my hand and when I moved to Mia's bedside, he moved closer to my brothers. Con reached for Aiden and took him from Grey, cuddling him into his chest. The anxiety was back; I was afraid of what my brothers would say to Grey now that we were apart.

Unfortunately—or fortunately, depending on how you looked at it—Mia stole my attention.

"Would you like to hold her?"

I smiled at my once again best friend. She looked tired but absolutely radiant. When Mia handed me my niece, I cuddled her close and lowered my face down to her sleeping one.

"Hello, little lady."

"Tell me," Mia said, her voice low. I looked over at her, a frown on my face. She lifted her brows and moved her head to the side slightly, signaling the boys. "Tell me!"

She scooted over on the bed, patting a spot next to her hip for me to sit and face her. I did as she wanted, keeping the baby between us and my attention on Ava's face.

"I love him."

"Awww."

I grinned to the side and looked up at Mia. "I have my reasons for keeping everything quiet. I know that that's probably going to irk Con and Rory, but most of it is going to stay between me and Grey."

"Grey?"

I grinned. "Yes, Grey. I stopped calling him Stone in private a long time ago."

"I love it. Tell me more."

Chuckling, I glanced back down at the baby in my arms, running a finger down her cheek.

I held Aiden at this age, but holding Ava, a baby girl, was hitting me a little bit harder. I took a moment to compose myself before looking back at Mia. "He's been my rock. I haven't always been the kindest. But he's been there, and he supports me. Heck," I said with a laugh, "he let me keep us a secret for this long. If I knew there wouldn't be fists flying, would I have been willing to share it sooner?" I glanced at the boys, who seemed to be more relaxed, if Grey's laughing was any indication. I turned my attention back to Mia and shrugged. "Maybe. But maybe not. Maybe the road we took is what we were supposed to take to get here. What's done is done and there's no reason to think about the what ifs."

"God, Bren. You're so fucking adorable." My eyes widened at Mia's swearing. She stopped swearing, at least in public, the month before Aiden was born.

Her eyes were misty. "I wish you would have felt comfortable telling me, but I understand why you needed to keep it to yourself."

Now I could feel *my* eyes getting misty. "Oh, Mia. Me keeping it from you had nothing to do with our past." Because that was where Mia was going with that comment. I knew it without a doubt in my mind. "It was more because I was afraid you'd tell Con."

Her laugh was a little watery. "Yeah, I probably would have."

CHAPTER THIRTEEN

BRENNA

Just like we had done when Aiden was born, Rory and I had a fruit bouquet and a meat and cheese tray catered into the room while family and friends filtered in and out through the late morning and early afternoon to meet the newest O'Gallagher. When the crowd was dying and it was down to just my brothers and I, as well as Mia, Grey, and the babies, I started to clean up what was left.

Grey walked up behind me and brushed his hand over the small of my back before leaning down and whispering in my ear. "I love you."

I smiled.

It was as if now that he'd said it and I responded in kind, he couldn't stop saying it. And I, well...I loved it.

"I love you too," I whispered over my shoulder, smiling when he pressed his lips to mine.

"No making out in corners, kids," Rory said, pocketing his cell in his back pocket. "Shoot! That's what you were doing the other day, wasn't it? You too like a little heat with your sweet." He chuckled to himself. "Ha. Poet and I didn't know it."

Conor groaned, shaking his head.

"No, we were just fighting that day," Grey told him, picking up a pile of paper plates and tossing them.

"Sure, sure..." Rory shook his head and walked over, snagging the last cantaloupe and pineapple flower from the bouquet before I could put the remaining fruit in a container.

"Speaking of fighting," I said, putting the lid on. I stacked it with the other container of what was left of the meat and cheese before turning to my brother. "I heard you and Emily got into a fight."

Rory took a bite of his flower and shrugged a shoulder, chewing slower than necessary.

"Yeah, I want to hear what's going on with you and Emily!" Mia shouted from the bed. Conor sat in a chair adjacent to her, his socked feet propped on the bed and Baby Ava bundled and curled at his shoulder. Aiden slept in the bed next to Mia.

"There's nothing to tell about me and Em," he finally said after finishing—yes, *finishing*—the fruit in his hand.

"You were awfully cozy with her at the dealership," Conor offered.

"But she was upset yesterday," I added, looking to Rory. "What did you do to her?"

"We just got into a disagreement, I said some words, she said some words, which echoed some words Con said—"

"Don't bring me into this."

Rory gave him a pointed look. "I just said she had words that were similar to ones you gave me." He shrugged again and turned to the containers, opening the meat and cheese to grab a cube of cheddar. "AndImaybeamgoingtomakesomechanges."

The room was quiet, everyone trying to process what Rory mumbled as he popped cheese into his mouth.

Mia, bless her pretty heart, said what we all wanted to. "Say that again, slower this time."

Rory groaned and looked up to the ceiling. "I'm going to make changes."

"For a girl?" Conor asked, his face splitting in a huge grin.

"Yes, for a girl."

Rory went to toss a cheese cube at him but Mia put her hand up. "Sleeping babies. You hit her with that, you will be hit with the wrath of Mia Hampton."

Rory pointed at her, palming the cube as he did. "Good point." Instead, he popped the cheese in his mouth.

By this point in the conversation, Grey pulled me to a chair and into his lap. I was surprised at the ease I felt. While Grey and I weren't *new*, putting us in this kind of environment was, and I would have assumed I'd feel some sort of unease, but I didn't.

My oldest brother shifted in his seat at Mia using her last name and I glanced at him, watching him. It wasn't a secret that he wanted to change Mia's name.

Just like it wasn't a secret that it would happen eventually.

But I knew he wanted it done sooner than later. He was so in love with her.

He caught me staring at him from across the room and raised his black brows. I felt like he was trying to tell me something, ask me something, but I couldn't figure it out.

Finally, he nodded his chin down toward Ava. "Av and I are going for a walk." He took his feet off the bed and put his shoes back on, one hand on the baby's back at all times. "You want to walk with me, Bren? You can be my hands." Then he addressed the room. "Anyone want a beverage?"

"You can leave her," Mia said with a frown.

Conor gave her a crooked grin before bending to kiss her on the lips.

"As her mama, you get her more than me. Just let me hold her for a little longer."

Mia smiled up at him and laughed lightly. "Ok, burly man."

He gave her one more kiss and rounded the bed. Grey patted my hip before I stood. I trailed my fingers over his shoulder and he took my hand when I was behind him. Pressing his lips to my knuckles, he let me go when Conor reached us.

Conor winked at me and slapped Grey on the shoulder in a friendly manner—it was still probably a bit harder than necessary—and walked with me out of the room, Ava still secure to his chest.

"Can't let her go, can you?" I asked my older brother, a big smile on my face. There was nothing like seeing him with his babies. He made such an awesome father.

His chuckle was quiet, his lips still pressed together, but Ava shifted on him at the slight movement. He turned his face into his daughter's and pressed a kiss to her forehead, walking with me in the otherwise quiet.

I pursed my lips in an action that was probably too duck face, so I quickly pulled my lips in. I sighed heavily as we walked to the open refreshment area. When he still said nothing, I stuffed my hands in my pockets.

Still, nothing.

"So," he finally offered the moment we reached the juice and water machines. "You and Stone. For five years."

Rather than feel the anxiety I imagined, I couldn't help but smile slightly at Con's voice. "Well, not really five years."

"That man back there has been dating you on the low for five years, Bren, regardless of when it was 'serious.'" He lifted his free hand to do air quotes and I couldn't stop my slight smile from filling all the way.

Conor wasn't an air quotes guy. Rory, sure, but not Conor.

"Why didn't either of you say anything?" One hand still on Ava, Conor opened a cupboard, revealing Styrofoam cups and lids. I reached in to grab them, knowing there was only so much he could do with Ava in his arms.

I shrugged, pulling down enough cups for our family. "I had some things I had to get over. Personal things."

I knew Con wouldn't be content with that answer. "Personal things? What, like all the rumors you lived through? Bren, you gotta know that none of that shi—stuff mattered."

I filled the cups, half with water and the rest with an assortment of the available juices. "It mattered to me. I wanted to make changes to who I was." I shrugged again, still filling cups. "For what it's worth, I said 'no' to Grey the first few times he asked."

"But eventually you said 'yes' and you still didn't feel the need to tell your brothers."

"I didn't want him to lose a job. O'Gallaghers needs a bartender like Grey, and that's not me being biased," I added with a pointed stare at my brother.

He let that go.

"But he's good to you." It wasn't a question; it was clearly a statement. I lidded a cup before looking at my oldest brother, the guardian of much of my youth, and took in his raised brows and concerned blue eyes.

I nodded once slowly and while my smile was much smaller, it felt like it had much more emotion behind it. "He's good to me."

"Then that's all I care about." Con opened another cupboard, taking down a disposable tray. I helped place the cups on it and when the task was complete, he and I headed back to the room.

Right before we reached the doorway, Conor stopped, his hand in his pocket and a frown marring his face.

"What's up?" I asked him, my back to the propped door.

His hand dug in his pocket for another second before he nodded, seemingly to himself. "Nothing. We're good."

Chuckling, I shook my head and pushed with my back through the door. "You're weird."

"Right back at'cha, Brenna."

STONE

I would have thought that the first time I was in the O'Gallaghers' presence after our announcement, with*out* Brenna, I'd have been uncomfortable to a degree.

Let's be honest. For as carefree as Rory sometimes acted, in the years I've known him, where his sister was concerned? He could be pretty fierce.

But it wasn't like that at all.

No, Mia and Rory joked with me like they did at the bar. Again, I found myself with Aiden in my arms, to which Rory took offense to.

"I'm the kid's uncle. You're not."

"Yeah, well..." I looked at Aiden and winked at the chubby ten-month old. "Give that a year."

Mia gasped. "Yeah?"

I shrugged, shaking my head at the same time. "Yeah. I'll give her time, though."

"Please not another five years."

I chuckled. "I said a year, Mia."

"Ah, yes. You did. Pregnancy brain."

"I don't know if you caught it, but pretty sure you *had* the baby already, Mi," Rory, ever the smartass, said.

"Fine. New baby brain." She stuck her tongue out at Rory. The teasing quickly turned to smiles as Brenna and Conor came back into the room. I stood to help Brenna with her full tray of drinks, giving Mia back her son, and taking the tray from Brenna to place it on the room's built-in desk.

Brenna, standing beside me, hugged me from the side and I wrapped my arm around her shoulders. "You good?" I whispered down to her. I could only imagine that her and Con's walk was more than just grabbing water and juice.

"I'm good," she answered, turning her smiling lips up toward me. I took the opportunity to kiss her lightly.

"Don't drop her..!"

Brenna and I collectively turned at Rory's voice, only to watch as Conor shook his head, readjusting Ava in his arms.

"I'm not going to drop my kid. She's not the first one."

"You weren't supposed to admit you dropped Aiden, Con," Mia whispered from the bed. My eyes swept to her, only to catch her laughing and holding up a hand. "I'm kidding!"

"I wouldn't drop my kid," Conor grumbled goodheartedly. "Rore, can you take Aiden please?"

Rory's auburn brows rose but he did as he was asked. "Sure. Hey, kid. It's your *real* uncle," he said, picking up the boy from Mia's side. Aiden babbled and pulled at Rory's hair, making him wince. "Yeah. Alright. Watch the hands."

"I think she's hungry," Conor said, offering a very much sleeping Ava to Mia.

Mia lifted a brow but accepted the baby. "She's sleeping, Con."

Conor shifted after standing. "Well...she was fussing a little out there."

Brenna shook her head against my side, her arms still wrapped around me. "N—" she started, but Conor cut her off with a glare.

Yeah.

A glare.

Like, she would have been struck by lightning if she dare speak a word otherwise.

"I love seeing you so concerned," Mia said, her words laced with laughter. She glanced around the room and shook her head before looking back down at her newest baby.

"We should probably start to get going though, so if she does wake up, you can do... you know, your thing," Rory said, waving toward Mia. "I've seen your boobs one time too many."

"Rory!" Brenna exclaimed but Mia only grinned at him.

"Hence the extra locks," Conor said. "You guys should stay for a few more minutes." He seemed fidgety. I had never seen the man anything other than overly secure in his spot in the world.

"Knocking works wonders too," Mia told Rory. Then, looking down at Ava, she added in a smaller voice, "Doesn't it, baby girl?" She brushed her finger down Ava's cheek, down her neck, and over her shoulder. Her finger caught on something under the blanket though and she turned her face up toward the group then Conor.

"Conor..."

He nodded at her, then gestured with his chin toward her hand. Mia placed Ava on the bed between her legs, slowly unwrapping the swaddle Ava was in. I felt Brenna jump slightly against me. Her excitement was coursing through her and I couldn't figure out—

"Oh!" Mia said, just as Conor lowered to a knee right next to the bed, reaching for Mia's left hand as her right picked up a ring that was in the swaddling blankets.

"Mia Hampton. You've made me the happiest man in the world, not once, but twice. Heck, a hundred and two times. I don't have a pretty speech because frankly, I'm a little afraid you'll shoot me down again but please. Please, Mia baby, will you marry me? Take the same last name our babies have? Let me love you forever?"

While I wasn't privy to all the details, I knew that this wasn't the first time he had asked, but I was pretty sure this was the most formal time he'd popped the question.

Brenna let go of me, only to move around and stand in front of me, leaning back. I wrapped my arms around her shoulders, loving that her chin rested on my forearms.

"Yes, Conor." It was whispered but it was through tears.

Conor shot up from his kneel, leaning into his now fiancée and mumbled against her lips, "Fuck yes," before kissing her soundly. It was almost embarrassing to watch.

"It's about time," Rory mumbled.

"You're next," Conor said, pulling back from Mia with a huge-assed grin on his face.

Rory shook his head. "Nah. I've got some time. But those two..." Rory pointed at us. "You shoulda heard Stone. He's planning on—"

"Close it," I told him. It took me five years to get Brenna to admit to us as a couple in public. I wasn't about to throw a proposal on her without talking through some things first.

Brenna grinned over her shoulder at me. "You're planning on what?"

I kissed her temple and shook my head. "We'll talk about it later."

I should have realized she'd never let it be.

"What were you planning?" she asked when I got into Mia's car after getting Aiden. We were headed back to Con's house for the moment. Brenna's mom and dad were sticking around the hospital for a little longer but then would meet us at Con's house and switch guard of Aiden.

I couldn't wait to get Brenna back to our place.

God, I missed her there, what with the last two times I went to bed and she wasn't there.

"Don't worry about it," I said around a chuckle, turning the ignition. "I'll tell you later." I looked over my shoulder, pulling out of our spot.

I caught Brenna looking at me, her brows up, before she looked in the back where Aiden was already fast asleep.

"God, I hope I have kids as good as Aiden," she said.

"You want to have more kids?" I asked her, glancing over her.

She nodded, still looking at Aiden, before turning her attention back to me. "I do. Holding Ava was a little hard, but there wasn't any room in that maternity suite for sad feelings of things that weren't meant to be." She offered me a smile and I reached over to take her hand, squeezing it once in support.

She squeezed mine back. "Do you?" She paused, as if weighing the silence. "Want kids? I mean, I know you said..."

It may not have been something I thought about at length before Brenna, but, "Yes. I do." I grinned over at her, winking once, before turning my attention back to the road.

"You know," she started, looking out her window. "Five years is a long time. And we *have* been living together for a year."

"Mmhmm." My lips tightened, the corners lifting.

"Maybe..." She glanced over at me then shook her head. "Never mind."

I let her have her silence, knowing without a doubt what she had on her mind—because it was on my own, too, and by the end of the day, I was going to ease her thoughts.

CHAPTER FOURTEEN

BRENNA

His hands roamed under my shirt, his tongue sweeping into my mouth. My own hands were fisted in his hair.

We made it back to our place a little bit ago and no sooner than walking into the duplex, Grey tossed me over his shoulder and headed for the stairs, carrying me up to the loft while I laughed into his back. Rather than tossing me on the bed though, he slowly dropped me to stand in front of him, my body rubbing against his deliciously on the way down.

"I love you, Brenna O'Gallagher," he said against my mouth, pulling back so he could lift my shirt over my head. I let go of his hair to allow him to do so. When it was off, I went to work on his jeans as he took off his own shirt. We undressed one another in hurried silence.

Still standing, he pulled my body close. I stood on tip-toe, my chest pressed to his, so I could pull his lips down to mine.

With our lips connected, he lifted me, an arm under my butt and the other banded around my back, and this time, brought me to the bed we shared—the one we spent many all-nighters in—to lay me down gently. I kept my arms wrapped around his neck, loving when he lowered his body to press mine into the bed.

I ran my toes up his calf slowly, causing his body to flex into mine. His hard cock trapped between our bodies twitched and I smiled into his mouth.

"You like that, do you?" he asked, a grin on his own face. Pulling back and kneeling between my legs, he grabbed his cock in his hand and slowly stroked his length. "Do you want this?"

"Yes, Grey," I said, but two could play this game. I shifted slightly, just enough to spread my legs more, and brought my fingers to my core, rubbing a slow circle over my tight clit. "Do you want this?"

"Fuck yes, baby." He squeezed himself once more and went to bring his mouth down to me but I covered myself with my hand completely.

"No, Grey. I just want you right now. I need you right now."

He pressed his lips to the back of my hand. "I need to taste you, Bren. God, I've missed this. Missed you."

I couldn't help the smile. "It was only two nights."

"Yeah." He kissed my hip bone. "Two nights where I stared at the ceiling hoping you'd come back to me."

I pushed up onto my elbows, peering down at him. "I'm sorry," I said softly.

"Don't be." He moved up to kiss between my breasts, making me lie back down. "You needed time. I got that. I pushed you, I should have expected it." His arms caged me again as he loomed over me, his face directly over mine. "But I'm not going anywhere."

I smiled up at him, reaching to place both my hands on his now day-old scruffy cheeks. "Thank you for being my rock. For not giving up on me."

"Never giving up on you, Angel," he said quietly as he lowered himself, his mouth closing over mine. We did some of his favorite "naked making out" before he reached for a condom at his bedside table where the boxes had lived, and had been utilized, since we began this adventure.

Thinking about our earlier conversation, I put a hand on his forearm to stop him.

He wanted babies. I wanted babies.

We should probably do things in the correct order, but I wasn't anywhere near my fertile window, and I was protected in other ways.

"We don't...have to use one," I shrugged, suddenly slightly self-conscious. Immediately, my head went through all the times I slept with men, some safely and others not. "I'm clean," I rushed on to add. And I was. Thank goodness for that, with my history.

He lowered his reach to place his elbow on my side, laying half on me, half off. With his other hand, he brushed wayward strands of hair from my face, staring down at me. "Are you sure?"

I nodded. "I'm clean."

His face split in the crooked grin of his that was incredibly endearing to me. "Angel, I wasn't questioning that."

I sunk into my pillow, slightly embarrassed that that was where my head went. "Ok."

He leaned into me again, licking the seam of my lips before kissing them once, sucking on my lower lip. "I know bareback isn't a big deal to some people, but it's a big deal to me," he offered.

"I'm sure," I whispered against his lips.

He moved himself over me again, lifting one of my legs as I did the same with the other, wrapping my ankles at his back. With slight guidance from his hand, he thrust into me, rocking us slowly at first, our mouths fused and kissing as slowly as our bodies moved with one another.

Eventually the pace picked up though and with my arms wrapped tightly around his neck, I pulled myself close and pressed my open-mouthed moans to his chest.

"Fucking...love...you," he said with each hard thrust in the mix of his short, quick ones. His hips moved against mine and I release my hold on his neck to hold on to his ass with one hand, feeling his muscle bunch with each quick thrust.

He rolled us, wrapping his arms around me this time, keeping me close and unable to sit up and ride him properly. With his feet bracing against the bed, he pounded up into me again and again.

I let out moans, most louder than the previous, as the feel of his corded cock continuously hit nerve endings in my pussy. I was so close.

With one of his arms banded around my hips and the other, my shoulders, I wasn't going anywhere. My open mouth was still pressed to his shoulder, my breaths coming out hot against his skin, the moisture from my breath mixing with his sweat. His grunts in my ear told me he was getting close too.

"Squeeze down on me. Squeeze, Angel. God, come all over my cock," he demanded between grunts.

I did what he asked, squeezing my muscles down around him, making the feel of him that much greater, sending me that much closer. Two, three, four more thrusts and my jaw dropped further and I fought to move my head to press my forehead to his shoulder. My moan as I came echoed through the duplex.

"God." Thrust. "Damn!" He thrust up into me one last time before his hot cum jetted inside my walls, his cock twitching and pulsing in me. "God, I love you, Brenna," he said against my ear, a shiver running through his body as his cock emptied.

STONE

Brenna lay in my arms, completely sated. I could do this for the rest of my life—love her, love on her, and hold her through the night.

Knowing what I wanted to do, I pulled away from her with a kiss and moved to the closet. Brenna sat up, holding the sheet to her chest for no reason other than the open windows in the place allowed a cool draft to circle through.

"What are you doing?" she asked as I went through a few of the boxes I had stashed back there, full of off-season clothing.

"Looking for something."

Before I moved in with her, I knew that this was the direction I wanted to take.

That Brenna was it for me.

Maybe it had been presumptuous of me, especially seeing as she hadn't allowed us to be in public for so many years, but I knew in my heart this day would eventually come. Finding what I was looking for, I took the ring from its box and carried it back with me, closed in under my fingers.

Brenna moved to sit against the headboard, watching as I returned to her. I tapped her legs and she folded them to her, allowing me to sit across from her. I kept one leg on the floor and the other folded between us, completely naked and not giving two shits about it.

"Brenna."

She turned her head and narrowed her eyes playfully at me. "Grey."

I grinned at her and held out my free hand for hers, which she placed in mine quickly. I squeezed her fingers, never taking my gaze from hers.

"You know I love you."

This time she grinned. "Yes. Yeah, Grey, I know. You know I love you, right?"

I lifted her hand to my lips to kiss her fingers. "Yes, Angel. I know." I kissed each finger before bringing our hands back down.

"I want to love you forever."

Her breath hitched and her fingers tightened in mine.

"I know you just got around to accepting who we are in public, but I'd love nothing more than for you to say you'll marry me. We can take our time; it doesn't have to be fast." I paused, actually fearful that she might say no.

But she smiled and there were tears in her eyes as she nodded her head. "Yes. Yes, I'd love to marry you, Greyson Stone."

My smile was the widest it had ever before gotten, I was sure. "Yeah? It's not too soon?"

Her smirk was cute and her words were mimicking. "It's been five effing years, Grey."

I chuckled, pulling her to me. She scrambled close, allowing the sheet to drop, and curled her body into mine.

"You did just get around to admitting us to your brothers, though."

"And they took it really well. I was worried for nothing." She traced her hand down from my shoulder to my closed fist.

Shit. My closed fist.

With a grin, I turned my fist upward and revealed the ring I had chosen for her two years before. I hadn't seen it in that time, but it was still as radiant, still as "Brenna" to me, as it was when I first bought it.

It was a simple square cut diamond, but the band had its

fair share of the brilliant stone too.

"It's beautiful," she whispered, staring at my hand. I leaned back from her so I could pick it up, holding it between us. "It reminded me of you. In a sea of all things radiant, you stand out. You always have."

She smiled, then bit her lip. "Put it on me?"

"With pleasure."

Then I slid the ring on its rightful home.

EPILOGUE

EIGHT YEARS LATER

BRENNA

"Bren! Come on, we're going to be late!" I heard as I scrambled to get the baby's bag together. At some point today, Chris, our eighteen-month old, thought it would be a really good idea to hide the baby's diaper bag.

I still couldn't find it.

So rather than continue to search for the missing bag, I was putting together a new one. I just couldn't find…

Aha!

I closed the closet in the nursery after finding one of Mikey's favorite two binkies.

They were all the same, but for whatever reason, the boy fell asleep better with one of these particular two.

"Bren! Angel, come on. The boys are getting antsy!"

"I'm coming!" I hollered back, running down the stairs to our renovated farm house. We moved a little way away from San Diego, but still close enough that we could go in to the pub when needed.

These days, I did a lot of the business minded things, while Con handled more of a human resources roll. We didn't need to both keep working at the pub; I could have left or he could have, but we both liked to keep busy. Grey had been the head trainer for many years, right up until we had Matt four years ago. He *asked* to be a stay at home dad.

Grey was not afraid of me being the breadwinner,

something that had me laughing a time or two.

I had two boys with black hair and gray eyes, but I was pretty sure baby Mikey's hair was going to keep turning lighter. I wasn't destined to hold another baby girl and call her mine; Grey and I were done having kids and I was completely ok with the fact I was going to be a boy mom. Nova was my baby girl and she'd always be my one and only.

When I rounded through the mud room, Grey was standing in the doorway with the door propped open, grinning at me. "You find what you were looking for?"

"I had to pack a bag! I told you this." I lifted the bag to show him.

"Why?" Grey frowned, allowing me to step past him and into the garage where the Pilot was running and waiting for us.

"Because Chris moved the other one. My goodness, Grey, I'd think *you* had baby brain." I shook my head and got into the passenger side, setting the bag between my feet.

Grey got into the driver's seat and shook his head, his face amused. "Chris didn't move the bag, Angel." Grey chuckled to himself and put the SUV into reverse, pulling out of the garage.

"He did! It was near the car seat and then it was gone. You know how Chris likes to move things." It was true. Many a pair of sunglasses and shoes have gone missing since Chris learned to walk.

And he started at ten months.

That was a lot of missing sunglasses and pair-less shoes.

Grey, still chuckling, hit the garage remote and moved the car into drive, heading toward the Bay. "No, Angel. *I* moved it."

I frowned. "But..."

"You never asked if I knew where it was. You would have saved

yourself a lot of trouble." Grey openly laughed at me now.

"You could have said something," I grumbled, crossing my arms and looking out the window.

Grey's hand wandered over and found its way to my thigh, squeezing gently. "You just said you were looking for something."

The smile was still evident in his voice, the bastard.

"Mmhm."

Again, he laughed. "Now we have two. You know," he paused and I could imagine him shrugging a shoulder. "In case Chris moves the one." I glanced over at him and he took the opportunity to wink at me.

He was mocking me.

The bastard.

"Mmhm," I repeated through tight lips, but I moved my hand to rest on top of his, intertwining our fingers when he turned his hand over to hold mine.

"So Con doesn't know? You're sure Mia didn't slip?"

I shook my head, looking back at my husband. "No. According to Mia he's completely clueless. Just thinks we're meeting him at the pub for a quick lunch."

Trying to surprise my oldest brother hadn't been an easy feat for Mia and me. Most of our ideas, Conor seemed to figure out but for whatever reason, when Mia told him about today's lunch, he hadn't batted an eye.

He was going to be surprised to see our parents there as they were supposed to be on another cross-country trip, but likely more because Rory, Emily, and their son would be there. Caleb and Sydney Prescott, too. We still wanted to keep it intimate so we kept our numbers low. There were also going to be ten littles running around, so we were trying to keep a pretty decent ratio of kids to adults. If we started inviting every employee and every close friend, the pub would be so full the littles would easily get lost.

"I don't know, Bren," Grey said, shaking his head. "I think he knows something's up. He was talking about seeing Rory and Emily."

I scoffed, shaking my own head. "No. I think he and Mia were talking about taking a vacation without the kids, and Scottsdale was the main idea."

"Either way," Grey retorted with a shrug, "it'll be good to see everyone. Hear any more news on the Prescott front?"

Caleb and Sydney didn't have family here, outside of Jonny

and the team, and because of that, they did a number of family dinners with Conor and Mia. Their kids got along incredibly well with Aiden, Ava, and Ali, but they hit a terrible rough patch recently.

My heart broke for them.

I shook my head. "No, but they did confirm they would come out with the boys for a little while."

"Good. They need an hour or two away," Grey said, nodding.

When we heard the news, Grey and I sat up all night talking about what we would do if we were in their shoes. It wasn't an easy place to put yourself.

I glanced over my shoulder, checking on our boys. All three were zonked out.

I turned back around with a small smile on my face.

No, I couldn't imagine what Caleb and Sydney were going through, but I wasn't taking a single day for granted.

STONE

I pulled our Pilot into the back lot just as Conor and Mia were getting out of their truck, Aiden and Ava arguing as they hopped down as well. Little Ali climbed down quietly, reaching for her mom's hand the moment her feet hit the gravel.

After parking, Brenna took care of Mikey's car seat, hauling him in it, and I unbuckled Matt, lifting him out of the SUV and allowing him to run to his mother.

God I loved calling Brenna that.

Wife, too. That was another favorite.

I walked to the other side to release a sleeping Chris from the confines of his car seat, hoisting him out and carrying the sleeping boy into the pub behind everyone else.

Brenna had placed the car seat with a still sleeping Mikey on a table, freeing her hands so she and Mia could pull a few of the lower tables together.

O'Gallaghers opening staff was already in, which worked perfectly with the plan. Con would never guess something was off, that the girls had actually pre-planned for the pub to be closed until three, leaving the place available to us for a few hours.

I looked at my watch before heading toward Conor, who was helping Aiden shoot darts in the back. It was my job to keep him distracted.

Thirty minutes, and it would be go time.

RORY

We were soaring above the sky, just reaching altitude. It would only be a matter of minutes before the plane began its descent once again. I looked out the window to see if I could make out the lights of the towns below

us as we flew through the dark sky.

It was a short flight home, only an hour, but Em hadn't thought she could handle sitting in a car for five and a half hours.

To be honest, I didn't think I could handle sitting in a car with her for five and half hours. She had to pee every twenty minutes. We would have never made it home.

I looked to my right where my wife of four years curled up beside me. She pulled up the arm rest to her right so she could pull her feet on the chair beside her, and the arm rest between us so she could lean into me. With my arm around her shoulders, she slept against me peacefully.

How she fell asleep so quickly was beyond me. One of the first times she did, I was in the middle of a conversation with her, post-sex, and thought she'd gotten pissed at me.

Nope. She'd only been sleeping.

I grinned at the memory, then reached for her hand resting on my thigh. I let my thumb play over the rings there before reaching further over to place my hand on her swollen belly.

I would be forever thankful for the chance she gave me.

After I first got to Arizona to be with her, she and I fell into a very easy rhythm, which surprised me. I had never lived with someone other than my siblings and Emily and I hadn't had a lot of alone time in the months, year, prior to me arriving.

I helped her study.

I walked the dog—that we ended up getting two months after I moved down and in. Sasha was a Golden Doodle, more golden than doodle, who definitely favored her mama to me, but was a sweet dog all the same.

Emily graduated from her CRNA program at the top of her class. I was so fucking proud of her. When she was looking at jobs, we discussed moving back home but then a position opened at the pediatric hospital she'd been working at, and it was her dream position, so we stayed.

Which was fine.

O'Gallaghers ran fine without me there—because, low and behold, my sneaky sister had more up her sleeve than just a secret relationship. Girl was a genius in business.

Not that I'd tell her that.

I took my weight loss, muscle gain, and supplement knowledge to a new level, and started my *own* company. It was a move that I questioned, as all of my clients were loyal to the company I found them in, but the move turned out to be a great one.

Between the two of us, Emily and I were able to move to one of the better neighborhoods in Scottsdale and on the day we moved into our home, I proposed.

She said yes.

If you hadn't caught that part yet.

We made a baby that day; I would swear that was the day of Will's conception until the day I died.

William Alexander O'Gallagher was every piece of his mother.

Oh, he was a hellion. He had to get something from me other than the waves in his white blond hair, but he was definitely Emily in a little boy package.

Emily shifted against me and I looked down, seeing she was still sleeping. I felt the baby kick and soothed my hand over the spot before falling back into my reverie.

It probably wasn't the most *ideal* being away from my siblings and parents while I had my own family starting, but it was working for now. Two weeks ago, my parents came and visited Em, Will, and I, staying in the house for a week before offering to drive Will with them to San Diego.

Emily and I took Will on a plane once.

Yeah.

We weren't doing it again for another few years.

I grinned at the thought. I loved knowing I had years and years of happiness ahead of me. Sure, I knew life could change in an instant but I wasn't going to do anything to change the path Emily and I were on. Did we have our fights? Absolutely.

But more than anything else, we had love and the love Emily had for me?

It was fucking amazing.

EMILY

When we landed in San Diego, we were met by my parents-in-law, who had our three year old box of mischief, Will, by the hand.

Will tugged on his Mamaw's hand until she let go, and he barreled his way toward us.

"Pick up your toes," I whispered with a grimace, seeing in my head him falling face first into the ground. It wouldn't be the first time if he did.

Rory chuckled beside me and rubbed the small of my back. I closed my eyes in brief ecstasy before Rory grunted. Opening my eyes, I knew what I'd witness.

Will launched himself at Rory's legs and now my husband was lifting him in the air, settling him in front of him as Will wrapped his little legs around Rory's hips.

"How's it going, little man? You be good with Mamaw and Papa?"

Will nodded. "Yes huh. I got a Paw 'trol toy. Wanna see?"

I ran my hand through his getting-too-long hair and we moved to meet up with Rory's parents.

"The drive was ok?" I asked them, even though I'd asked them the same thing the other day when they made it to their hotel.

"It was," Rory's mom reassured me with a smile before hugging me. "And the flight? How's this one holding up?" She put her hands on my ever-growing belly. I was thirty weeks but so ready to have this baby.

"Baby's well."

"Everyone's at the pub and waiting on us," Rory's dad said, breaking in. It was Conor's fortieth birthday and we were having a get-together for it.

According to Mia and Brenna, Conor didn't know so that would be fun.

I reached my hand out toward Rory, who took it more than willingly. Then, as three, my little family followed Rory's parents.

CONOR

My wife was up to something. She'd been co-conspiring with Brenna for the last few weeks and every time I'd ask or say I knew what was up, Mia promptly denied it.

"Bullseye!" the board's robotic voice said, and I looked down to see my boy doing a dance in his spot. He had no moves.

Chuckling, I ruffled his hair. "Good job, Aiden."

I let him be, checking on Ava at the pinball table, her five-year-old sister Ali looking on. When she shooed me away with her hand, I grinned and joined Stone and his boys.

"They're up to something," I told him as I took a chair, turning I backward, and sat down. My eyes were on my wife and sister at the bar, whispering something to Jon, the cook who was working our opening shift a little later.

Stone, with a bored look on his face, just shook his head. "Those two are always up to something."

"Isn't that the damn truth," I mumbled.

Suddenly there was a lot of commotion.

I glanced over my shoulder at the sound of music playing from the kitchen and watched as my parents walked, in followed by...

"No fucking way," I said around a grin, standing.

Remembering I was near my nephews, I grimaced to Stone. "Sorry, man." He just chuckled and stood but I didn't pay any attention to him from there. My kid brother was home.

We saw Rory and Em usually about once a year, but this was definitely a surprise. I walked over to them and pulled Rory into a hug, grinning and patting him on the back. "Hey, kid. What brings you back?"

My nephew Will wiggled from Rory's arms to be let down, scrambling to join Matt and Chris.

"Hey, Em," I told her next, leaning in to kiss her forehead. "You look ready to pop."

She smiled, her face absolutely lighting up. "Don't I wish."

"That baby's cookin' for another ten weeks. Don't jinx it," Rory said, pointing at me.

I chuckled but went back to my earlier question, "Seriously though. What brings you home?"

Then the commotion was at the front of the bar and I turned and watched as Caleb and Sydney Prescott and their brood of boys came through the doors, their youngest baby girl held in Caleb's arms. My friends looked tired but the fact they were here instead of where they likely had been before?

Something was definitely up.

Before I could question it, the music changed, this time to fucking Happy Birthday.

I turned in a circle, taking in my family and friends before my eyes landing on my wife, standing by Brenna. I playfully glared at her and stalked toward her. The music was loud and everyone was singing, but it didn't stop me from leaning down at talking in her ear, "I told you no birthday shit."

She smiled up at me, that beautiful fucking smile that still knocked me in the gut after ten years. "You only turn forty once, old man."

I groaned at the reminder, but my groan was quickly replaced when Mia's lips found their way to mine.

"Happy birthday, lover," she spoke against my lips.

I smiled against hers. "Thank you, Mia baby."

MIA

Our time was wrapping up.

I was happy with how things turned out. Brenna and I managed to surprise Con, something I wasn't sure was possible.

I looked around, taking in our family and friends, seeing everyone so happy.

Even Cael and Sydney had smiles on their face, as Sydney had a sleeping two-year-old Brooks on her lap, her chin resting on his brown hair, while Caleb held their youngest, Braelyn. Brody and Brandon were playing with Aiden, but it didn't miss my attention every time Cael or Sydney's eyes lingered on one of their babies longer than normal.

My heart broke into a thousand little pieces every time I saw Sydney look at my girls, knowing that I couldn't help fix her hurt. That nothing I could do, nothing Con could do, could help their family.

I liked to think that this helped, getting their family out and moving. It was probably hard, but I hoped it was at least healthy for them.

Before tears could burn my eyes, I moved to my husband, hugging him from behind. He angled his body so he could reach behind him, curling an arm around me and bringing me to his side.

"Thank you, Mia," he said, bringing his lips down to my ear, the beard he still wore to this day, tickling against my ear.

"For?" I snuggled into his side.

"Everything, Mia baby. Everything."

Did you enjoy Brenna and Stone's story?
Please consider leaving a review on Amazon!
Also, be sure to check out the Troublemakers: Mignon
Mykel's reader group on Facebook!

Continue reading for a look at
Interference—Caleb and Sydney's story!

INTERFERENCE

CALEB

I shouldn't have gone to O'Gallaghers with Jonny last night.

I pulled my pillow from under my head and, face planting into the mattress, pushed the sides as close to my ears as possible. Anything to block out the annoying ring of my cell phone.

Last night, San Diego won. As was tradition, Jon Jon and I went out on the town. Sometimes the other guys on the team would come along but for the most part, it was just me and the kid brother. Back in our peewee hockey days, mom would take us to McDonald's; in college, the one year he and I attended at the same time, we would party in my dorm. Now, we went out, partied long and hard, and of course, shut it down. Most of the bartenders looked the other way with some of the younger athletes in town, and we could always count on Conor O'Gallagher. Rumor had it the O'Gallaghers were a little rough around the edges. Probably why Conor was willing to overlook Jonny not quite being twenty-one yet.

Both Jonny and I had been drafted to the San Diego Enforcers. During my senior year of college, Jonny's freshman year, we both walked into training camp as college kids with great stats, and walked out with spots on the roster. Sure, the Prescott name means something to the organization, but Jonny was a damn good goaltender, and my stats were better than dad's in the respect he didn't touch majors until he was in his mid-twenties, having played in the American league for a few years beforehand.

Last night's win meant the Enforcers were that much closer to Sir Stanley and his Cup. Finals were well within our reach. All we had to do was win Tuesday night's game and we'd make it into the next round. It was a close series, but the odds were in our favor. With Jonny in net, Vegas had to pull all the punches to get the puck past him.

I sighed blissfully when my phone finally stopped ringing, but just as I was about to drop off that sharp edge of sleep, Jonny slammed my bedroom door open. I lifted the pillow enough to look over my shoulder at the intrusion, watching as my boxer-clad brother tossed the cordless house phone onto my bed, bouncing off my hamstring–a little too close for comfort.

"Fucking asshole."

Jonny merely raised a dark blond brow. Oh, the perks of sharing a condo with your younger brother.

I guess it could be worse. My sisters weren't exactly the easiest to live with.

"Next time, wake up and answer your damn phone," Jonny grumbled. "There's a lady on the other end, and I don't think she much appreciated my sarcasm."

I reached back for the phone with one hand as I tossed the pillow aside with the other, before shooting Jonny the bird. As I put the phone to my ear, I watched my twenty-year old brother shuffle back toward his own room. "Caleb," I said on the exhale of a tired sigh.

"Um, hi," came the voice on the other end. Female, like Jonny said. Not high pitched, but not as sexy and throaty as some female voices were. Nervous, maybe. I didn't think I knew her voice, and the landline number was pretty locked down, so she couldn't be some weird stalker chick. I squeezed my eyes shut briefly. Way too much thinking for this hour.

"I'm so sorry that this seems to be an inopportune time. I figured you'd be up and moving, as it's ten." Was it ten already? "I thought that was the time you started practice on game days. I'm on a tight deadline and was really hoping to just leave a message." Ah, she didn't expect to actually talk to me.

"And this is…" I stated, not asked, before yawning.

"I'm sorry," she apologized again. "My name is Sydney Meadows and I'm calling on behalf of Sorenson Media Group. I tried to reach you through your agent, but he directed me straight to you."

I made a mental note to talk to Mark the first chance I got. He really needed to stop directing people to me. Wasn't that his job? To figure out what appearances and gigs were best for his athletes when they weren't doing what they were being paid to do? Fuck, Mark knew I didn't like to sign up for the extra things that came with being a pro-athlete. Events with the team, sure. Gigs at the rink, absolutely. But beyond that, it was a hard no.

"We are putting together a reality television series, and you are one of the names we were interested in having involved with the show," she stated in a rehearsed manner.

I didn't think sleep was going be coming back to me anytime soon, so I rolled over onto my back before throwing my legs over the side of the bed. As I stood, I shook my head. "Yeah, sorry. No reality TV."

"If you'd just let me pitch it to you—"

"That's all you're going to be doing, Miss Meadows. Do you really want to waste your breath? I'm not doing television."

"That's fine," she rushed to say. As she began talking about multiple women and just as many dates, I strode naked to my dresser to pull out a pair of old, worn sweatpants. I pulled them on while listening with one ear. She continued to talk, so I continued to move, walking out of my room and down the hall that was home to both mine and Jonny's rooms, a spare room, and a bathroom, before walking barefooted down the stairs. Whenever she'd pause for an answer, I was sure to give a barely verbal 'mmhm' just so she would continue her rant and be closer to done.

I had sisters. I knew how to work a phone call with the long-winded female species.

"So great," she said finally, with a smile evident in her voice, so unlike the unsure tone at the beginning of our conversation, one-sided as it mostly was. "I will meet you tonight after your game. Thank you so much, Caleb. I promise you, you won't be disappointed."

Standing in front of the fridge now, I frowned when I heard the telltale sign of her ending the call. I pulled the phone from my ear only to stare down at the 'call ended' screen, the frown not going anywhere.

Well shit...

What did I just agree to?

AVAILABLE NOW!

ABOUT MIGNON MYKEL

Mignon Mykel is the author of the Love In All Places series.
When not sitting at Starbucks writing whatever her characters
tell her to, you can find her hiking in the mountains of Arizona.
Mignon writes in one world, so while every series can be read as
a standalone, her stories will be more enjoyable if you read them
in publication order.

LOVE IN ALL PLACES *series*
full series reading order

Interference **(Prescott Family)**
O'Gallagher Nights: The Complete Series
Troublemaker **(Prescott Family)** *
Saving Grace **(Loving Meadows)**
Breakaway **(Prescott Family)** *
Altercation **(Prescott Family)** *
27: Dropping the Gloves **(Enforcers of San Diego)**
32: Refuse to Lose **(Enforcers of San Diego)**
Holding **(Prescott Family)** *
A Holiday for the Books **(Prescott Family)**
25: Angels and Assists **(Enforcers of San Diego)**
From the Beginning **(Prescott Family)**

** The Playmaker Duet (Troublemaker, Breakaway, Altercation, Holding)
can be enjoyed in one easy boxed set.*

Printed in Great Britain
by Amazon